The Ascent of Isaac Steward

MIKE FRENCH

To John

Mike

Published by

Cauliay Publishing & Distribution
PO Box 12076
Aberdeen
AB16 9AL
www.cauliaybooks.com

First Edition
ISBN 978-0-9568810-1-4
Copyright © Mike French 2011
Cover design by © Vicky Delfosse

A CIP catalogue record for this book is available from the British Library.

Dedication

My dad, Jeffery French, for believing in me enough to brave reading a novel

Acknowledgments

I try to avoid lists as they usually involve me having to do stuff like shopping, mending the fence or packing for holiday. But here we go ... a big thank you to all these wonderful people that helped in many different ways to bring this book to life...

Vicky Roberts, Andy Roberts, Paul Burman, Helen Corner, Kathleen Maher, Charlie Wykes, Sue Hall, Paul Bridle, Brian Hutton, Jenny Whitehouse, Mum & Dad.

And

Tabitha and Joel for helping choose the final cover.

Matthew for showing me the secret of happiness.

Michael Molden who ended my six year period of walking around half-mad in the wilderness looking for a publisher.

A special thank you to Vicky Delfosse for the cover artwork and to my wife, Emma for supporting me in what must be one of the strangest but most rewarding of endeavours.

Mike French
May 2011
www.**mikefrench**uk.com

Contents

Prologue

Isaac reached out towards the rock face. It felt cold yet he could sense warmth buried deep below. Particles of rock shifted, mica clustered and the mountain tried to find the form to fit the impression of skin pressed against it. Isaac looked out across the canyon and waited until he was sure that the rock and he had become one. A hollow formed across the granite; Isaac pressed in his hand blurring the boundary between flesh and stone.

The winter sun played with the canvas below finding its way into nooks and crannies, moss and hollows; painting a yellow hue that was insipid; the promise of warmth withheld until the earth tipped a nod to its God. Clouds swept over the top of the mountain range. Isaac watched a buzzard glide on the thermals then pulled up on his handhold and set his climbing shoes against the smooth face.

A wind crept around from the north and flowed either side of Isaac, outlining his shape in movement. He stopped and felt it against his cheeks. Forming solid edges to his hand again, he found definition in his blue tipped fingers and raised his head. He could smell pollen, bluebells against water, snowdrops through snow. Images of movement came with the wind: children, trains, butterflies, boots revealing grit under virgin snow.

Isaac swept aside the memories and focused again on being still so he could see in his mind's eye the position of the window he had seen in his dream. He slowed his breathing and saw himself falling. Isaac blinked and looked around: the beauty of the open space calmed him and he pushed his fear into the ends of his toes.

He looked up. The clouds grew darker, the wind left him, the smell of promised spring left his nostrils, the buzzard became two, then three, then one continuous circle of flight.

And then in the stillness, high above, just to the right, Isaac saw the window.

Isaac pulled his dream around him and felt his insides become fluid. Everything seemed transient to him, nothing within was still, his organs became water, his bones white froth on blood.

He set out and the rock itself became fluid as Isaac swam through towards his goal. Gravity span in confusion and tugged one way, then another. The stone kept him close, embracing Isaac in its form, protecting him from the consequence of separation. At points Isaac's body seemed to sink into the mountain, but he kept his eyes ever on the end before him.

He surfaced just below the window. Made of wood, it was grafted onto the mountain. Rust fell as orange rain from the contorted railings running along the front of the ledge. Isaac looked as the buzzard swooped down and perched on it. It turned its head, met his eyes then flew off again. Isaac's pulse increased, his hand now clammy. He reached for the handle to open the window. Inside he could see a family gathered around a breakfast table, behind them a large tree set in a woodland.

Isaac felt heavy as if a stone falling through water to the bed below. His head span; his fingers started to come away from the handle.

'Open it,' he thought. 'Open it.'

Tears formed in his eyes, sweat swept his brow and formed a sheen on his hands. He drew back.

In his dream, he had fallen. Screaming had given way to silence as his body snapped and pulped. He'd sunk into the dust, as if the ground was quicksand. Isaac remembered the dirt flowing into his mouth, finding the hollows inside. Choking. Darkness. The never ending darkness.

Act 1
The Awake of Dawn

Chapter 1
Night is Coming

The back of Isaac's retina fired signals towards his brain. For a moment he rejected them, acting like a stubborn child refusing to sit up at the family dinner table. Music sounded like the on hold music piped down phone lines to encourage callers to disconnect. A test card image of a girl, chalk in hand, grinning clown beside her, filled Isaac's view. Forty years of senses refused to accept the scene, like an old castle wall confused as to how hold defence against the march of National Trust feet. Then the chatter of his children.

Isaac swept aside the test card girl, the radio replaced the piped music. His sense of smell gave in next: chocolate, cut grass, flowers. Touch: pitted indents in a wooden table under his fingers caused by the children, foreign bodies pulled in to wreck destruction. Taste: pizza at the back of his throat.

Isaac swallowed and gave in. Around him were his wife, Rebekah, and his children, Jacob and Esau. They sat around a large circular oak table; a planet around which family life orbited. On the wall were pictures of the children taken at school marking for posterity their rise from sand pits to spelling to sport. Isaac looked at Rebekah; candles sparkled before her set on cake marking his birthday.

Jacob shifted in his chair and fiddled with his hair. Esau's eyes widened at the sight of cake, Rebekah broke into song. For a moment it was a solo rendition of happy birthday, then the backing choir joined her, and they sang the hymn to time, praising it for dragging Isaac to forty.

Isaac leant forward and blew out the candles.

'Happy birthday,' said Rebekah and raising a knife cut down into the layers of sponge.

Jacob picked up his glass of lemonade, 'Cheers!'

Esau groaned and felt for his cup, Rebekah smiled and nodded at Jacob.

'To Dad,' said Jacob.

'To Dad,' said Esau.

Isaac sipped his champagne, 'To me and to my family.'

'I need the toilet,' said Esau. He scrapped back his chair and headed out.

Jacob finished his cake and looked at his Mum. Rebekah carved off another slice and passed it over to him.

Isaac looked down at his cake. When he looked up the day had passed, the children were in bed and he stood in the evening looking at Jacob's crayon man. A broad smile sat offset beneath its blue eyes, as if existing beyond the confines of the rounded face. Written below were the words *we love you Dad*. Isaac ran his finger over the words, then tapped the mercury filled column of the glass thermometer next to it. The silver thread slipped indicating the drop in temperature. Ten degrees. Isaac stuffed his hands into his jacket pocket and fumbled around until he found his stubby pencil and notebook. Flipping it open, he scribbled down the information to join the mass of data charting the history of his garden in the language of Fahrenheit and Celsius. He pocketed the book, took the thermometer from the wall, and wiped an old cloth over its surface.

The hard beam of a flashlight illuminated Isaac's face as he polished the wood set around the instrument. He finished and looked up. The dim light of the evening flowed over his angular brow and down his nose. Isaac smiled as he felt the vastness of the sky above tug at his sense of wonder. He placed the thermometer back on its rusty nail and turned off the flashlight. With no light to compete with, the evening hues increased and soaked Isaac and his garden in soft focus. A gentle breeze caressed the pink blossom of the cherry trees and the noises of the day made their way home, blanketing the scene in reflective slumber.

The sun slipped under the horizon. Orange and pale yellow glows washed around the impression left in the sky. The evening colours flowed down to follow the warmth, striating the sky into darkening blues. Isaac leaned on his walking stick as a warmth, which defied the cold evening air, flowed into him.

Images of stars across the horizon twinkled in his eyes as he watched the darkness claim the sky.

Rebekah approached Isaac.

'Pull this around you, Isaac, it's getting cold.'

Isaac folded his arms around Rebekah and pulled her in. Laughing, she rubbed her nose up against his in an Eskimo kiss. Isaac moved his head over to the side of her soft cheek and whispered in her ear, 'Shall we play Eskimos later?'

She smiled back at him and squeezed his hand.

'Without the kissing, your beard scratches me.'

'Rebekah, you know how I feel about-'

Isaac felt her finger on his lips. She pushed herself up onto her toes, replaced her finger with a kiss, then walked back to the house. Moments later she returned with two steaming mugs of hot chocolate and setting herself beside Isaac, snuggled up into the security of his embrace.

After a while, she sat up and turning, peered into the pale slate blue of Isaac's eyes. Within them she saw the reflection of the stars spiralling away into their depths; she giggled, laid back again, 'Let's play our game.'

Isaac nodded and reaching down fumbled for the lever on the chair. CLUNK. The back of the chair reclined tipping Isaac and Rebekah backwards.

'Our garden rollercoaster,' said Isaac.

'Keep your hands in at all times,' said Rebekah.

They laughed, then as they lay sandwiched between the sleeping soil and the wandering night, Isaac started to paint tales of aged years against the darkened sky. Words threaded their way in and out of the clusters of stars until the image of a white wood formed above them.

'Where is the Dandelion Tree?' said Rebekah.

'In the middle. Right at the centre of things,' said Isaac.

'Can you still remember?'

'Yes,' said Isaac.

'Then tell me. If you can see it, describe it.'

'It's like no other tree that ever lived,' said Isaac. 'It towers over the white canopy, large and majestic. Other trees gather at a respectful distance, glad only to fall in the shade of its branches. The trunk rises straight and true like a great ship's mast.'

'I can see it … there are dark bands encircling the trunk,' said Rebekah. 'Like corset strings straining to hold back the years.'

'Corset strings? Hmm … I suppose.'

'It takes a women to see things as they really are,' said Rebekah.

Isaac laughed.

'Okay, there are *corset strings* around its smooth white bark. The branches fan out from the top, like wooden fingers spread across the sky. Smaller branches push out and entwine to form a latticed bowl. There's a long rope ladder that my father made from honey brown English yew, carved into smiling crocodiles, and two old sailors' ropes.'

'Which now flash dusty grins at our visitors,' said Rebekah.

'When I was five-years-old,' said Isaac, 'I thought the tree looked like a dandelion seed which had lodged itself into the ground and then forgotten it was supposed to turn into a dandelion. Instead it shot up into a massive seed shaped tree. I used to wonder what would happen if it remembered it was a dandelion. Would it grow into an enormous yellow skyscraper to be seen for thousands of miles?'

'Put yourself in the tree,' said Rebekah.

'I am seven-years-old and I sit cupped in the wooden branches. The wind blows my hair. I feel like a Prince surveying the kingdom I will one day inherit. I can see scrub flowing out from the edge of the wood formed by sunken trees, which breathe by pushing the tips of their branches up out of the ground. There is a field between the wood and the house, which is covered in the stubble of an unshaven sleeping giant.'

'Stubble Face Field.'

'I look down and see tall swishing grasses against the trunk. Birds sing around me, there is a sweet aroma from the broad evergreen leaves.'

'Don't forget the daffodils,' said Rebekah.

Isaac smiled, became quiet then said, 'But you don't believe, when I told you what I saw there-'

'What has that got to do with it? I don't have to believe to enjoy listening.'

Rebekah held Isaac tight, thought for a moment, then said, 'Come on, let's go there now.'

'But it's dark, why?'

For the second time that evening she pressed her fingers onto his lips.

'Shh, come on.'

He nodded. The couple got to their feet and set off towards the edge of Stubble Face Field. They walked in the light thrown from the house until they reached a point where it faded, leaving them in darkness as they approached Mamre Wood. Isaac flicked on his flashlight as they entered. The path was dry and crunchy. As they pushed in they became surrounded by a sea of bluebells which swirled around the trees and lapped up to the path's edge. Unknown to them in the shelter of the wood, the breeze started to turn stronger and blew in immense clouds from the north, which scraped the ground and tugged at the sky with rounded heads.

An owl hooted above and span its neck round to follow them. They glanced up, eyes searching. Two dots of light shone out from the thickets. A fox. On they trudged until the trees closed in around their heads and framed them in a wooden arch. The entangled architecture drew them to a soft glow of light set in the distance before them. As they neared the moonlit scene, the wood pulled back and a clearing, encircled by sycamores, stood before them.

Isaac flicked off his flashlight. A ring of daffodils sat upon a large hummock in the clearing. The ground at their centre was gashed in an open wound, exposing an earthen cavity. Isaac and Rebekah stood together, held by the scene. Rebekah turned towards Isaac.

'Give me your knife.'

Isaac fumbled around in his pocket, pulled out a little carving knife his dad had given him, and passed it over. Rebekah clasped the knife in her long fingers and stepped forward into the circle. Stooping down she cut a daffodil and gave it to Isaac.

Isaac smiled and hugged her. Rebekah swung her arms up around his neck and nestled herself into his chest. The yellow daffodil followed the line of Rebekah's back in the embrace.

Moments passed. The night seemed to hold its breath. A drop of water landed on the daffodil. It rolled around the trumpet, then continued on its fated journey; a teardrop shed at the passing moment. Another drop fell, then another, until lines of water hatched down surrounding their bodies in blue.

Isaac looked up, the rain tickled his eyes and he smiled. He grasped hold of Rebekah's hand and whispered into her ear. Laughing they dodged back through the rain. It hit the undergrowth around them and swept up a chorus of muffled notes into the night air.

Reaching the house, they bolted inside and shook themselves. Water droplets scampered over the smooth surface of the wooden floor beneath their feet. Rain pitted down into the two cups of forgotten chocolate. Skins floated to the top and slid over the red glaze into the grass.

Hours later, the daffodil sat drinking in the cool water in the china vase on the sideboard. Evening had moved into night. A log from the Dandelion Tree burned in the hearth. Rebekah lay asleep. Isaac stood in the bathroom. The rain continued to fall, and blown by the wind, tapped at the bathroom window. The old wooden frames creaked. Outside, a leaking gutter sent drips falling towards the patio marking out, in their repetitive sound, the ticking of a clock. Drip, drip, drip. Isaac stood listening to the sound of the rain on his house. The old grandfather clock in the hall joined in the marking of time and chimed ten o'clock.

Isaac waited for the chimes to finish, then, running his hand over his thick beard examined his face in the bathroom mirror. Reaching up into the cabinet, he pulled out a pair of scissors. He looked at the glint of metal for a moment, then attacked his beard, hacking away the years of growth. Thick curls of hair fell into the sink and onto the tiled floor until the hard edges of his chin started to show and his beard became stubble. He stooped down, gathered the hair up and pushed it into the pedal bin beside his foot. The brutal attack left no signs of sadness in his face. Instead, his mouth twitched, then spread out in a wide smile.

Isaac turned on the hot and cold taps and swilled the two waters together to fill the bowl. Cupping his hands, he leant down and splashed his face. Drops fell from the tip of his nose. He pushed past the medicines into the back of the cabinet and pulled out his shaving brush, razor and soap bowl. His actions were uncertain as he swirled his brush, scoring pieces of soap up into the bristles. He lathered his stubble, picked up his razor. Pulling his skin taut to accept the cut, he brought down the blade.

As he worked, Isaac's mind wandered and he recalled his first experience of shaving. It happened when his parents bought him a British Navy Action Man. Isaac had unwrapped it, looked at its beard, then cried. A week later, Isaac presented the toy to them, now an SAS Commander with a black jump suit and body armour. The biggest difference, however, was the face itself.

'Dad, look I shaved him!'

Toothpaste had formed the lather over the offending growth, a razor blade had shaven it all off.

Isaac finished shaving, refilled the sink and scooped up the cold water to his skin. Pores closed at the shock. He picked a thirteen-year-old box of Old Spice, and took out the opaque glass bottle. Tipping it upside down he poured the after shave into his hands and rubbed it over his face. It stung. Isaac swore. He glanced around the doorframe at Rebekah. She was still asleep. Returning to the mirror, he watched a spot of blood appear, and another and another, until it looked like ants playing paintball had wandered onto his jaw and discharged all their red paint pellets over his face.

Isaac grabbed some tissues, ripped them into pieces and squashed the ants.

The passing of time continued, keeping step with the grandfather clock and the leaking gutter, until the clock chimed eleven o'clock. Isaac sat in the chair beside his bed. The light from a small lamp threw his face into sharp contrast. His right hand side was illuminated, showing the upturned corners of his mouth; his left-hand side was in complete darkness. As he stirred, he turned causing his face to slip further into the night. On his lap lay a well-thumbed copy of Steinbeck's 'To A God Unknown' open at the last page. He snored. The noise slipped under the door and filled the upstairs landing with its life beat.

The weather outside grew worse. The wind whipped itself up into a frenzy and blustered around the garden. Isaac and Rebekah slept on. High up in the sky, thunder roared like the sound of rushing water cascading down a ravine. Raindrops broke into tiny shards of water and splintered off to different altitudes in the storm. Lightning flashes raced over the bottom of the clouds, illuminating their bases as they searched for the area over Mamre Wood.

As they neared it, the flashes grew violent and rapid, strobing the night in brilliant flashes of light. Each lit the darkness for a brief second, and in those moments the window appeared in the sky. Strange images of winged creatures with faces made up of men, eagles, oxen, and lions raced forward through its panes. The lightning forked radially inward, setting the sky ablaze with fire. The atmosphere strained as it became charged then, when it could stand it no longer, the air gave way and lightning cracked downwards searching out the place where the Dandelion Tree had once stood.

A thin tracer raced upwards from the broken ground, jagging its way through the charged atmosphere to join the downward bolt. High above the ring of daffodils they met each other, and with its downward journey confirmed, the lightning struck with a reddish glow, searing the open wound.

Chapter 2
In the Beginning

The morning mist hovered over the expanse of water. Below streams of bubbles writhed in perpetual turmoil.

Dark nightmares of the mind.

Sleeping gunk in the corner of his eyes, body in a state of morning confusion, Isaac started to wake. Around the bed lay sheets of yesterday's newspaper, a lizard skin shed from the past; beneath them the centrefold spread of a Playboy.

Isaac turned off his radio, formed two star shapes with his open fingers and sat up. He rubbed his eyes. He felt heavy, as if an astronaut returning to earth finding his weight.

It was six thirty in the morning.

Isaac gave into gravity and as he laid back onto his sweat soaked pillow a fragment of his dream caught at the edge of his mind.

'What was it about?'

Isaac felt the dream slipping away.

'No,' said Isaac. 'It was about a tree, a family, a window…'

He glanced up at the flaking paint on the bedroom ceiling, then sat back up. Images of his mother, Sarah projected before him onto the calico curtains.

She lay on the floor of a supermarket with packets of lentil soup around her. Isaac stood as a boy over her. A man in a tatty red and black cloak with a tear running up the front of it was laughing as he kicked Sarah with his black boots.

'No, Fable, please,' screamed Sarah.

'Matilda Mother!' said the man.

Isaac looked away as the man smashed a can of baked beans into her face, his cloak flapped around him straining at the old medal pinning the material around his neck.

Isaac glanced back. Sarah's face was mangled, blood and beans pooled around her.

'God.'

Isaac got out of bed and paced around the room. He stopped and watched bubbles rise through the warm water of his tropical fish tank. Orange and black striped Clown Loaches swam around the air stone sitting on the gravel bed. Isaac looked above and stared at the paint samples on wall, left from a time when there was a chance the room would get decorated before the perpetual fatigue of parenthood. Nothing else registered, familiarity had cloaked the landscape with an invisible sheen.

Isaac stooped down and looked at the Clown Loaches. The long elliptical leaves of an Amazon swordplant swished in the turbulence. There were five Clown Loaches in the tank; Isaac saw only four. The kids had named them: Rebekah, Isaac, Jacob, Esau, and Ishmael. The last one at the protest of Isaac; the kids had pleaded with him after a weekend at Granddads.

The memory of Ishmael, his half-brother, floated to the top of Isaac's mind.

Four fish became five at the back of his retina.

'Ishmael?'

Isaac reached up to his face and felt the scar below his right eye. The sound of bubbles in the tank became the patter of rain.

A flash of a blade, blood, a cry of fear filled Isaac's mind; he looked at the tank; the water became turbulent, then, turned red. The liquid crystal thermometer changed colour as it ascending its scale. Isaac closed his eyes. It was a memory he had made a decision to forget, to erase from his mind. Yet here it was tormenting him.

Isaac opened his eyes; the fish tank changed from red to blue, the rage subsided.

Adjusting himself within his boxer shorts, he opened a drawer under the tank and took out a small net. Pushing it past the Java moss he swept up a Clown Loach into the mesh. Isaac tipped the fish into his hand and stared at it. The four Clown Loaches left behind hid under the rocks at the back of the tank. Two sharp spines pierced the skin of Isaac's hand.

'Shit.'

He carried the Clown Loach out of his bedroom and into the bathroom. He looked at it one last time, then tossed it into the toilet. The fish span in the water under the peach blossom sanitary block as Isaac relieved his bladder.

He kicked his boxers off into the corner and stepped into the shower.

Showering was a risky business in Isaac's house; he saw it as a kind of aquatic Russian Roulette. He stood shivering under the showerhead; span the dial around on the control, as if a chamber to a pistol pointed to his head, and pressed the *On* button. He tensed, waiting. A few drops of water formed from the surface of the showerhead and rolled around its rim. Half way round they met each other, joined forces to gain weight and dropped onto Isaac's head. He looked up to see if that was all the shower had to offer.

Up to that point, Isaac's face had remained crumpled by his sleep, as if it hadn't decided which expressions to use that day. Now his eyebrows twitched into life and went downwards to meet his sleepy blue eyes. He clenched his fists causing the pink bits of his knuckles to slink off down his fingers, raised his arm and battered the shower control.

'You're pathetic,' he shouted at the shower as if it cared.

There was a loud rumble, then a pencil-sized column of water drilled out. Isaac stepped into it and started rubbing a small hard piece of soap over his body.

'Jane Peter,' he said trying the words on his lips, 'Jane Peter.'

They had met at the pub last night. It had felt thrilling as if he was a boy again unravelling the line to his birthday kite: releasing the virgin canvas to the wind. They had talked for hours. Then there was the cinema:

'Would you like to see Mona Lisa Smile?'

'What?'

'It's a film, would you like to go see a film?'

'I ... er, okay, what the hell.'

'Do you like popcorn?'

'Love it.'

Isaac felt the side of his face where she had kissed him before they said goodbye at her front door.

'Jane Peter. J-a-n-e Peter.'

Bubbles ran over his legs, swirled around his toes and disappeared down the plastic plughole.

The water stopped; Isaac gave up and got out of the shower still covered in soap. He dried himself and squeezed some toothpaste onto his toothbrush. Wrapping the towel around his waist, he walked out of the bathroom brushing his teeth. Reaching the end of the landing, he placed his hand against a door with a sign: **No Adults: Keep Out!**

Isaac pushed open the door and stepped inside. He looked around, breaking the hushed silence of the room with the whirling noise of his electric toothbrush. Like every morning, he checked to see if everything was in its right place; the books strewn across the floor, half the toys out of their boxes, the bed with sheets pushed back, a pillow under its slatted boards on the floor. And each time Isaac felt the rise of an emotion, he balanced himself with words. Stripped of their meaning, they formed a mantra of the Clown Loach names to soothe him ...

Rebekah, Isaac, Jacob, Esau.

Rebekah, Isaac, Jacob, Esau.

The rhythm filled his mind, the ting of a tuning fork, blocking the chaos of connection with reality. He felt calm. Orange and black fish swam through his mind, protected by the environment of the aquarium.

Rebekah, Isaac, Jacob, Esau.

Rebekah, Isaac, Jacob, Esau.

Isaac shut the door, returned to the bathroom and spat into the sink. He placed his toothbrush down and picked the gunk out of his eyes. Then he walked into his bedroom, threw the towel on the floor and pulled on a clean pair of boxer shorts.

'Shave,' he said almost as a command to himself and returned to the bathroom.

He rubbed the condensation from the mirror and flicked on the small strip light above it. He ruffled his short, brown hair that shot off in all directions as if charged by the night's sleep.

'Shave.'

Isaac picked up his electric shaver.

Reaching up, he slotted the two-pin plug into the shaver point. It smiled at him with its little shaving face. Isaac ignored it and flicked up the switch on his shaver. He ran it over his chin in the predetermined flight pattern it followed every morning. As it entered into autopilot it buzzed away like a satisfied bee on nectar. Stubble disappeared into its inner crevices, revealing pore pits left from a painful youth under the whirl of the shaver head.

Isaac's mind started bubbling as a micro snowstorm of hair settled on the smooth enamelled sink below his chin.

'How can I solve the bug in my genetic programming causing my hair to sprout out like Plasticine through a sieve? It's like mown grass, it just keeps growing back.'

Images of Isaac slaughtering his electric sheep in the dead of night rose.

He finished shaving his reddening face, bent down and span open the tap. He chased the hairs around the basin, encouraging them to join the swirling water, then leaned into the mirror, and rubbed his hands over his chin.

Isaac's crow's feet radiating out from the edge of his eyes wrinkled together. Creases appeared around his mouth, pushing themselves back into his face. His eyebrows moved up causing furrows to appear on his forehead; he dropped his jaw, stuck out his tongue. His face softened and the ripples on his forehead receded back down; his eyes filled with light and he felt the release of laughter rise within.

The memory of Jacob drawn by the lure of a father's joy, replayed in Isaac's mind. Isaac shielded his eyes as the glare of the sun sent rays up through the plughole of the sink. The hard tiles of the floor became sand. The sink grew; its curves straightened out forming the long line of the horizon.

'Jacob?' Isaac thought as he saw his son stumbling towards him, the white of the enamel glaring behind him.

The light twinkling within him faded.

A tear rose up and dropped down into a well-worn channel in Isaac's face. He turned, walked out of the bathroom and went downstairs chanting,

Rebekah, Isaac, Jacob, Esau.

Rebekah, Isaac, Jacob, Esau.

Opening the back door, he stepped out into the garden, naked apart from his boxer shorts. Goose bumps rose up over his skin. With long wet grass under his feet he walked towards the flowerbed at the back of the garden. The spotlight bolted to the house, switched on and threw a pool of light over his hunched shoulders.

Isaac stopped under the charcoal sky and looked at Mamre Wood in the distance.

He rocked backwards and forwards,

Rebekah, Isaac, Jacob, Esau.

Rebekah, Isaac, Jacob, Esau.

After an hour of this Isaac returned to his kitchen and walked towards the fridge. He stopped at its white door and read the messages there spelt out in magnetic letters. Isaac pulled open the door; the words blurred across his vision and disappeared. Inside, lurking in the darkness, sat the fridge light, its filament twisted, charred and broken waiting to be replaced. Isaac reached in past the eggs and butter and took out a plastic lunch box. He turned, stepped towards the bin and peeled back the Tupperware lid. A sandwich, a packet of crisps and a yoghurt tumbled out as he turned it upside down. They landed in the detritus of Isaac's solo existence.

He returned to the fridge and took out the butter and some cheese. Opening a packet of sliced bread, Isaac placed two pieces onto the work surface. He scraped a knife over the surface of the butter and like a lathe over wood, shaved off a curl. The bread protested and snagged as Isaac turned the white yellow. He worked the butter into the bottom corners of the bread, then followed the curve of the top of the bread in one smooth sweep of the knife. Cheese followed, then the top slice of bread; a cut through the middle and the sandwich was complete. He wrapped it in cling film and placed it in the lunch box.

Isaac opened a cupboard door, pulled out a purple packet of crisps and set it down beside the sandwich. He returned to the fridge to look for a yogurt. None. Sighing, he went to a shelf, took a piece of chalk and wrote on the kitchen blackboard: *yoghurts for Jacob.*

Isaac closed the lunch box and set it on the middle shelf in the fridge. He closed the door: the hum of the fridge retreated, leaving the house quiet as if in mourning. The sound of Isaac's breathing filled his head; he rubbed his eyes with his fingers and stood fixed for a moment by the sight of dirty dishes pushing up towards the ceiling: a man-made monstrosity, a tower that needed to be torn down by a hand other than his.

Chapter 3
Take Captive Every Thought

Jidlaph sat deep below the surface of Isaac's consciousness. Before him bubbles passed through the light cast into the darkness by the lanterns of the Subconscious Tavern. He turned as the tavern door swung open. Ripples flowed through the fluid filled interior. A sentry looked up and spun a domino between his fingers.

A young man, wearing a long overcoat and a rolo with trim hat, swam through. Jidlaph shrank back into the darkness and watched. The sentry clinked his double six domino down onto the table and nodded at the man. The man pulled the collars to his coat up around his neck and leant against the bar.

'Ten pints of Memento Melt and a Benco Belch, extra chilled.'

Behind him a chrome jukebox squatted on the floor; the aural displacement of Morrissey's 'First Of The Gang To Die,' rippled out through a blue arc. The bartender looked at him as he pulled down on the tap. A red sticky fluid glooped down into a dirty glass. The man stared back for a moment, then turned and examined the sentries' muskets lying in the rack against the far wall.

'That will be two bubs, Laban,' said the bartender when he had finished.

Laban took the Benco Belch, downed it, burped, and inserted two bubbles into a small circular opening in the top of the bar. There was a loud sucking noise and they disappeared. Laban grabbed the tray before the bartender could complain and made his way to his favourite seat next to the huge viewing window. As he passed the toilets, a sentry, bent double over his zipper, knocked into him. A glass fell from the tray and shattered on the floor; broken edges floated across the room and thudded into the double top of the tavern's dartboard.

'Sorry,' said Laban.

The sentry looked up, his old eyes unfocused.

'Can you help me?'

'What,' said Laban, 'with …'

A sentry sitting at the table opposite looked across. Lying across the table was a young woman dressed only in newspaper. The sentry tapped his lead pencil on the table and glared at Laban.

'Okay, okay,' said Laban.

He set the tray down and helped the old man pull up his flies.

'Thank you sonny.'

Laban brushed his hands down the side of his trousers, then picked the tray back up and made it to his table. Raising a glass, he looked at the bubbles rising within his drink; each formed an outline of a girl that danced as she rose. Laban tipped them into his mouth and took a long thirsty gulp.

'Oh that tastes good,' he thought. 'Goodbye unwanted memories.'

As he drank, he peered out through the viewing window, watching the water outside. Thousands of bubbles drifted up. Taking a packet of cigarettes from his coat, Laban tapped one out and lit it. Smiling he sat back on his chair, rested his boots on the table and blew a smoke bubble towards the ceiling.

'I thought you had given those up,' said Jidlaph emerging from the shadows.

Laban spat out a jet of Memento Melt. The droplets floated across the room and splattered into a table against the far wall. The table sucked up the fluid, then forgetting what it was doing there, rose up and floated up out of the tavern.

'Hello, Uncle,' said Laban stubbing out his cigarette, 'I … it was just the one.'

'It's good to see you, Laban, you've been keeping busy?'

'Yes, there have been a lot of break outs recently.'

'Arh … yes,' said Jidlaph, 'these are lucrative times for a bounty hunter.'

'Who do you think is responsible?' said Laban.

'There is talk that Ishmael has come under the influence of Fable.'

'Hmm.' Laban watched a school of large bubble rings bounce together like dodgem cars in the fluid outside, 'I couldn't make contact with you.'

'It has been difficult,' Jidlaph leant forward and whispered in Laban's ear. 'There are rumours that Rebekah will return.'

'After all this time? How do you know this?'

'There is a path along the woodland stream,' said Jidlaph, 'It is where your father escaped.'

'Bethuel's Leap? It exists?'

'Yes, and there lies our hope.'

Laban glanced across at the bartender. He downed his pint, wiped the froth from his mouth, 'Another drink?'

Jidlaph nodded. Laban looked at the bartender again.

'Here,' he said turning away, 'have one of mine.'

Laban stared back out of the window and watched the bubbles outside swarm together to form the shape of a small boy. The boy's face had two flushed circles set around an upturned mouth and cobalt blue eyes. The child turned towards him, waved, and swam upwards. Laban watched him ascend. The boy approached the surface, kicked hard through the smooth membrane, and broke through.

'Flipp'n heck,' said Laban, 'he made it. Uncle, did you see that?'

Jidlaph nodded, 'It was Jacob, look there is Ishmael as a young boy.'

'What is going on, Uncle?'

'It has started.'

Ishmael swam past the Subconscious Tavern and disappeared. He materialised again at a synaptic junction inside the neuron skyways that weaved their way through the upper limits of Isaac's mind. Neurotransmitters raced past him carrying memories to Isaac's long term memory. Ishmael followed them drawn on by the current that drove through the fluid filled tunnel. Finally, breathless he arrived.

A vast circular black surface spread out before him. Rising up at its centre, far off in the distance stood a white monolithic tower. Neurotransmitters were parked up in rows around it like the gathering of cars outside an Ikea. Memories stretched out in a line away from him.

'Welcome back to hell,' thought Ishmael.

He looked at the barrier that blocked his way. A small kiosk stood behind it. He watched as the door opened and the memory of Jacob, swam out. Jacob glanced around, then seeing Ishmael darted away.

'One of Isaac's stupid kids,' thought Ishmael, 'where is Fable?'

Ishmael ducked under the barrier and swam over the long stay parking lot towards the tower.

As he drew closer he could see thousands of portals that peppered the outside of the prison. One of which was the window to the cell that held him for thirteen years. The hair on the back of his neck prickled as he thought of his time there. Flinching at the chill in the fluid surrounding the tower, Ishmael slipped past the memories waiting to be processed and passed through a portcullis with the words ... HM TEMPORAL GYRUS ... spelt out in neon letters above it.

A large circular courtyard opened up before him. Ishmael peered up through the shaft that brought mist swirling down to a ceramic floor. Before him stood a hundred and one stone columns each with a door in flaking blue behind it set into the curving wall of the courtyard. Ishmael swam up to the only door that was red. Pigments of paint suspended in the fluid swirled around his toes as he kicked. Behind the door he could hear voices.

'Take your clothes off.'

Ishmael glanced over his shoulder, then, placed his ear against the door.

'No, cup your hands like a gorilla beating its chest, it makes a better sound.'

Whack whack; laughter.

'Would you like a blow job?'

29

Ishmael placed his hand against the door as groaning seeped through the grain.

At the sound of a voice behind him, Ishmael stepped back and flattened against the stone column.

'Got toys,' said Jacob as he passed by. 'SQUEAKY. BOING. SQUEAKY. BOING. SPLAT.' Laughter.

Ishmael swam back out and watched the toddler pass under the portcullis. A neurotransmitter pulled up beside Jacob with a screech. He got in, dropping a plastic frog onto the floor. Behind Ishmael bubbles appeared as the red door started to open. The neurotransmitter drove off with Jacob giggling in the back.

'Back in ancient Greece, our ancestors classified humans as laughing animals.'

Ishmael turned; Fable stood smiling in the open doorway, 'Hello, Outcast.'

'Fable! You scared the shit out of me, what were you doing in there?'

'Shh, follow me.'

Fable led Ishmael back out under the gate. Ishmael looked at the memories now lined up before the prison wall. Four Clown Loach fish darted around Jidlaph who stood back in the shadows watching. Behind the memories swam girls dressed only in sheets of translucent newspaper, their hair billowing in the current.

'Who are they?' asked Ishmael, his eyes widening.

'Temporal prostitutes,' said Fable.

'What?'

'The images in Isaac's Playboy magazines become prostitutes in his mind here, they serve the sentries and er-'

Fable coughed, 'and others.'

'But the sentries are old men.'

'True, most have erectile dysfunction and five foot muskets instead, but they enjoy reading the newspapers wrapped around the naked bodies.'

'O, I see.'

'Hush now, Ishmael, you are too young for such things, watch …'

A red glow formed in the darkness over the parking lot. The light streaked out vertically and a creature materialised in a large circular aperture in the wall. Tentacles writhed from its body, one snaked out and four groups of four orbs pushed their way through the transparent convex membrane at its tip.

'It's Abimelech, one of the three custodians,' said Fable.

'Remember our deal,' said Ishmael, 'you promised to kill Isaac's mother and get me to the beach.'

'Corporal Clegg!' said Fable, 'Calm down, Sarah's dead, the beach awaits you.'

The custodian moved towards the memories outside Temporal Gyrus, propelled by the swishing of his long tail. Bubbles streamed out like spawned sperm across the walls from the motion. Abimelech stopped and floated whilst his orbs span around him. Finally he spoke, 'Welcome.'

'Why did I have to come back here?' whispered Ishmael.

'I have one more job for you,' said Fable.

'What?'

'Shh.'

The custodian extended his head and looked up and down the line.

'Isaac's mother was murdered last night, after escaping the confines of these walls.' Abimelech's orbs glowed red. 'I will find out who did this atrocity and when I do ...'

The orbs changed from red to green to blue, then disappeared. Jidlaph stepped forward, opened his eyes and let the images before him record in his memory. Earth fell back from a mound, the sound of bone against bone rippled out through the fluid.

'This will happen to you,' said Abimelech.

Ishmael watched as the skeleton of a seagull rose, its wings flapped, its beak snapped up and down and a shriek like that of a mother running to catch her child from the edge of an abyss tore at his ears. The Temporal prostitutes screamed.

'Julia Dream! Time to leave,' said Fable as the seagull swam up over their heads and disappeared into the mist.

'What the hell just happened?' said Ishmael.

'He's changed a memory into a Relic Monger; it will feed off the memories that try to escape.'

'Like us?'

'Come on.'

Ishmael remained still, transfixed by the custodian. Jidlaph withdrew back into the shadows.

'I consider all of you a potential threat to Isaac's well being,' said Abimelech. 'Being locked up here will not make you a better memory, you will be released again only if I decide you will benefit Isaac's state of mind.'

'Come on.' Fable grabbed Ishmael.

Ishmael glanced back as they swam into the prison. Behind him, he could still hear the voice of the custodian, 'Once inside you will be compressed into smaller memory audio files to ease overcrowding. That means you will only be able to speak one key phrase that identifies -'

'You shouldn't listen,' said Fable. 'He has the voice of siren.'

They headed towards a large opening in the middle of the floor in the courtyard. Around them bubbles floated up as a hundred doors opened in unison, sending out a wash of blue. Behind them the voice of a sentry commanded,

'Sentries step forward.'

A sentry appeared at each door and marched out, each bringing his boots down onto the floor with a click as they stepped in front of their stone pillar.

'Attention.'

A hundred muskets settled against ancient shoulders. Newspaper floated out from the open doors, naked girls swam out and spiralled upwards around the pillars.

'Stand at ease.'

'Quick,' said Fable and disappeared down the hole in the floor with Ishmael in his wake.

Isaac closed the flaking red door to the larder and set the washing up liquid bottle down beside the tower of dishes. He span open the tap, filled the bowl with water, then squirted the liquid from the bottle over the dishes.

Picking up his cereal bowl and a piece of toast, he turned and walked across the ceramic floor. He left the kitchen through a hole where there should have been a doorway; a rough-cut of stone waiting for the day that plaster and wood would finish the job. Isaac looked at the toast, then bit into it as he made his way back upstairs. Dry crumbs fell from his mouth and dropped onto the stairs leaving a trail to guide him back, should he become lost in the labyrinth of his mind. Hung on the wall was a picture of Rebekah and Isaac caught in soft focus in digital pixels.

Isaac pushed open his bedroom door and returned to his cocoon. He set down the bowl of cornflakes on the dressing table. It joined the mass of food that sat there as if Isaac was a bear hoarding a store for hibernation. Stooping down he pushed aside the newspaper on the floor and picked up the copy of Playboy. Sitting on the bed he flicked through the pages. He stopped at a girl that fitted the spaces in his mind, a key cut to fit the holes in a lock. Nothing happened behind the cotton of his boxer shorts. Sighing he tossed the magazine down and picking up the paper flipped through the pages to the crossword.

In his mind, Fable and Ishmael swam through a dark tunnel. Small mouths nipped at their feet, sheets of newspaper floated across them; the sound of girls giggling seeped into their ears. They reached the end and rose up into a large canteen area.

It was deserted. A large willow tree stood in the centre. Blue spotlights played on the underside of the willow, Angel Fish nibbled loose bark floating up like leprous skin, barnacles encrusted exposed roots.

'What else do I have to do?' said Ishmael.

'In a short time, the custodians will release what they classify as a happy memory into Isaac's mind.'

'What is it?'

'A Punch and Judy show he saw as a kid.'

Fable paused and watched the chains holding down the willow tree clink.

'I want you to kill them when they reach the beach.'

'No, I don't want them with me down there,' said Ishmael, 'I have plans.'

'So you'd better kill them when they arrive then,' said Fable pushing past the swing doors of the canteen into a corridor. Ishmael clenched his fists and considered plunging the knife in his pocket into Fable's head.

'They are here at the moment.'

Fable pointed to the cell blocks either side of them, the sound of *'That's the way to do it!'* floated out of one of them and echoed in the dark.

'Why won't they end back up in here after the recall?' said Ishmael.

'Fandango,' came the sound from another cell.

'Same reason you haven't,' said Fable, 'things can be arranged.'

'There'll be a hangin', sounded from the cell behind Fable.

'Fable?' said Ishmael and looked around. Fable had disappeared. A blue light appeared from out of the darkness. A custodian swam out from it; Phicol unravelled one of his tentacles and tapped the bars.

Clang. Clang. Clang.

The sound flowed around Ishmael.

'Hello,' said Phicol looking at Ishmael. 'What have we got here then?'

'There'll be a hangin'

'That's the way to do it!'

It was at this moment that Isaac started sending urgent requests to his brain. As a result of the demand, the other two custodians gathered together in the upper level of Temporal Gyrus.

'Report from the sentries,' said Abimelech, 'they have located the file in Upper CellBlock C1400.'

'Pulse regulators are straining to keep Isaac's heart beat within normal parameters,' said Ahuzzath.

'Then there's no choice,' said Abimelech. 'Authorising early release of happy memory on medical grounds.'

The two custodians looked into the stream in front of them. The water was crystal clear. The liquid flowed out of a portal in the sidewall of the room, passed in front of them, then exited the room through another portal. Bubbles streamed through it. Clusters came together to form words.

...Reintegration to consciousness will be achieved without problem ...Confirm memory extraction from Gyrus. Exiting neural skyway at junction twenty. Entering bio-data light portal now...Download into subconscious sixty percent complete. Estimated time for completion: 30 seconds...

'Where the hell is it?' said Isaac...

Please hold...

'I hate it when I can't find my book,' said Isaac.

...Download complete. A bubble has located and incorporated memory. Ascending now. Re-encasing port...BEEP. BEEP. BEEP.

The stream turned red, a warning alarm sounded...

Warning: Escape of category A high-risk memory during release procedure. Memory fragment is highly dangerous and unstable. Ninety percent probability of a serious breakdown of normal activities if the prisoner manages an unauthorised entry to consciousness...

'Do we have enough cortisol available?' said Ahuzzath.

'No, they've run dry with all the breakouts recently,' said Abimelech.

'Better dispatch Laban into the subconscious instead.'

'I hope he's sober this morning.'

Chapter 4
There Before Me

Darkness flowed above the floor, shrouding it in secrets. Nothing moved. Strewn across the landscape were things long forgotten. A few lay remembering their days on the outside; most had lived in the shadowlands for so long that dust blanketed them in despair and they could no longer remember the light through the etched glass.

Many had been ensnared into this land without hope, and yet still the darkness was unsatisfied and it reached out with long fingers to snatch more.

A different set of fingers reached into this world, 'Aha, found you.' Isaac picked up his book from under his bed. Balancing it on his lap he started to read as he munched away on his Cornflakes. They crunched, or would have done if he'd bothered to eat them downstairs. Instead the soggy mush entered his mouth without any sound effects to enhance the flavour.

Isaac finished his breakfast and closed the book. He walked to the window, hesitated at the calico curtains then pulled the material back. Peering through his reflection at the grey morning outside, he listened to the end of the news on his radio …

'… we will bring you updates on the situation at the airport as they come in. Weather now. The strong storms affecting the region last night, have now finally moved on. The weather today will be dominated by an area of low pressure sitting over the region. It will be generally overcast with heavy showers, clearing this afternoon, when there will be some periods of sunshine. There will be a light southwestly wind and temperatures will reach a maximum of sixteen degrees Celsius, which is sixty-one Fahrenheit.'

An old woman passed by, who stooped as if carrying the weight of her years in the handbag clasped before her. She smiled and said 'hello dear' to a young girl with a bulge of stomach showing beneath her top. Isaac looked at the girl and wondered if it was too many morning muffins or time at the house of fun that had pushed her tummy out over her mini skirt.

A car drove past the girl, flashed at a car approaching from the other direction and pulled over. Isaac pondered at the custom of blinding people to signal safe passage. Images passed of the old woman pulling a knife from her handbag and sticking it into the muffin girl's eyes as an act of kindness, before stepping to the side of the pavement to allow her past.

Isaac blurred the world and focused on his reflection cast over the etched design of a tree. The world moved on as he stood motionless trying to find the strength to face such a land. Eventually he turned and made his way downstairs. He opened the front door and walked towards the safety of his Porsche 911 Carrera Cabriolet. He turned the handle, then looked up, as the postwoman walked down the brick paved drive.

'Morning, Mr Steward.'

'Morning,' said Isaac, looking at her. She had a large postbag thrown over her back, the thick strap across her chest, a ponytail bobbed behind her.

'How are you today?' she said handing him a large envelope. Isaac examined it; it was the latest House Beautiful magazine.

'Fine, just fine … couldn't be better.'

'Good, busy day ahead at the office?' she said walking back.

'Hmm? O yes, busy day,' said Isaac smiling.

Isaac turned, unlocked the front door and placed the magazine with the rest of the unopened magazines in the utility room. They stood there stacked and unread; the subscription running on as he stood still.

Isaac walked back out. The postwoman was still there, chatting to someone at the end of the drive. He got into his car and turned on the ignition.

Click.

Isaac's car radio strummed into life and pumped out through the ten speaker sound system. Isaac turned it up. The music responded by thumping around the car like a school bully, shaking everything not bolted down. Flicking open the glove box, he pulled out his sunglasses and in the grey of the blue morning, slipped on his shades.

Isaac pushed a button. The top of his convertible folded back into the rear in response. With the roof gone, the sky flowed down into the car. A family of sparrows overhead spotted the up currents of music and swooped down. As they neared the car they spread their wings and rode the rising notes high up into the sky to join the passing planes.

Isaac flipped another switch and watched the spoiler rise up from the back in his rear view mirror. Looking at the postwoman, he pumped some fumes out of the twin egg shaped exhausts and released the hand brake. The shiny alloy wheels turned and the ocean blue car rolled out past her into the street.

With three hundred horsepower and a top speed of one hundred and seventy eight miles per hour, the car nudged along in the traffic. John Trench, who lived nearby, always got to Tamarisk before Isaac and would greet him with a coffee in hand, bicycle clips around his ankles. There would be no such race today: John was heading for the airport, Isaac to the city hospital.

'And later,' thought Isaac, 'later Jane Peter.'

Isaac watched the exhaust fumes rise in the cold air creating patterns that his mind tried to find shape in. They swirled up into the trees, pumped by feet on accelerators with nowhere to go, so that the cars looked like trains backing up a track, smoke billowing as tempers flared.

Back at the house, Isaac's answer phone clicked on and downloaded its memory from the past into the present ...

'Hello, you have reached the home of Isaac, Rebekah, Jacob and Esau. Please leave a message. Thank you.'

Whirl ... Beep beep ...

Click.

Rebekah hung up.

The flight of sparrows disappeared behind clouds. Below, the Porsche's needle nudged past ten miles per hour. A crawling car in front spat a spray of water globules towards Isaac from two sky bound washer nozzles. Isaac cleared his windscreen with a single stroke of his wiper blades.

Drizzle started to fall. Isaac ignored it and leaving the top down, continued to weave his way through town. Tall overhanging lime trees lined the street around him.

Stationary again.

Isaac drummed the dashboard. Three years ago he had regularly driven his Porsche on this route to take his sons to nursery. He remembered the morning scramble to get ready - kicking feet resisting the bow of laces; teeth, toast, trousers. All had eaten away at time with a veracious appetite leaving him late and flustered. Isaac looked at the clock again. Above him the trees rustled in the breeze and spoke to each other in whispers.

Drip. A cold drop of water fell from a tree and slid down the back of Isaac's neck.

Drip. Another drop hit the top of his sunglasses; it slid down obscuring his view.

Isaac wiped away the water from his lenses and pulled away. The trees cast dark reflections onto him and as he picked up speed, his face went in and out of the black shadows flowing over the windscreen.

In the corner of his eye, Isaac saw a newspaper flutter across the pavement. The wind picked it up and gutter press swarmed across the road. It flew up in front of the car and plastered over the wet windscreen. Isaac's world went black and white. Reaching around, he pulled the newspaper from the screen and hit the brakes hard as a roundabout reared up before him.

Isaac watched as car after car pulled on from his right. He wondered if a factory, just out of sight around the corner, was churning out thousands of cars from its production line onto the roundabout. He remembered being stuck here during his nursery runs. Once, an old man had frightened the life out of him here by tapping on his windscreen …

'Behind you sonny, would you take a look behind you.'

'What?'

Isaac recalled turning and looking at his one-year-old, smiling in the small back seat of his Porsche.

'Yes, cute isn't he.'

'No lad, on the road, on the road.'

Isaac got out and looked at the squeaky toys strewn over the road. Jacob had thrown them out of the convertible. With the music player up full blast, Isaac had been unaware of the …

SQUEAKY. BOING. SQUEAKY. BOING. SPLAT of the toys as they had shot out to meet their death under slow motion wheels.

'What the fuck are you doing?'

Isaac snapped back from his memory and got to his feet.

'Sorry, sorry, just …'

Isaac looked around. He had been scrambling around on the asphalt under the car behind him.

The honking of horns sounded. Isaac could hear the man talking to his wife as he got back into his Porsche, 'This is what happens when you let mental cases loose in the community,' he raised his voice towards Isaac. 'They should be locked away, padded cell mate, padded cell.'

More honking of horns.

Isaac pulled onto the roundabout, cutting several cars up, his heart thumping.

He drove on past a row of elder trees along a park; the sound of 'padded cell' ringing in his ears. High above him a lone magpie followed. It looked down with beady eyes. Isaac glanced up in despair as more red taillights before him flared, and for a moment the image of two magpies appeared, one in each lens of his rain dashed sunglasses.

Daylight flowed through the glass of Isaac's bedroom window. It cast a blue shade of the etched tree on the windowpane over his bedspread. Specks of dust danced in the sunbeams; they disappeared as a shadow fell over the room. A face appeared on the other side of the window. The darkness under the bed withdrew, muttering, 'Gabriel, Gabriel.'

There was a sucking noise, as air withdrew from the room. Gabriel started to pass through the window. The glass bowed, trying to pull him back outside. Unused to flowing at such a rate, it shattered, sending thousands of tiny shards shooting into the bedroom. Pieces tore through the space-time forming the bed as if it were only tissue paper; time bled out from around the gashes in the mattress and flowed up. With millions of displaced minutes contained within it, the room slowed. Some leaked out of the window and landed around a young man who checked his watch; it showed four in the morning. He trudged back to his house and curled up into bed.

Gabriel looked around; his long white linen jacket creasing at his waist. Well tailored with smart gold buttons, it had a stiff-necked collar that underpinned his face. Gabriel's hair, cropped short, was as white as snow. Deep within his eyes, an orange light flickered, a blazing fire. Around his feet, a blinding light shone out, glowing like a furnace. The shards of glass reflected the luminance, sending thin shafts of light, criss-crossing the bedroom.

Glancing down Gabriel saw Isaac's book lying in a pool of glass on the bed. He picked it up and started to read:

The Beginning.

In the beginning God created the heavens and the earth. And lo the government pulled it all down as he didn't have a building permit. God saw that this was not good and marched, full of wrath, down to the town council hall. But it was a Sunday and closed.

The blazing fire in Gabriel's eyes turned a deep blue. He tossed the book back onto the glass bed and looked up. Mouthing a few words he tipped back his head, then laughed. The sound, rich and deep, roared around the room, a noise of rushing water. On and on it sounded, soaking the bedroom in joy. Tears formed at the edges of Gabriel's eyes.

The laughter broke against the bedroom walls, flowed back under Gabriel's feet and swelled up underneath the windowsill.

As he continued in his joy, the level of laughter increased until it rose up high enough to pour out of the window. It cascaded down onto the brick below, roaring like the sound of a great waterfall, and rolled down the drive into the unexpectant passers by. They stopped and soaked in merriment.

And then Gabriel stopped. The dreariness of the morning enveloped the street again and the crowd that had gathered fell silent.

Gabriel turned, held his hands upwards and closed his burning eyes.

Time passed. A warm wind rose up outside. At first it was gentle, and sent the rubbish scurrying along the pavement, soon it grew strong. The crowd fought to stand against it but it picked each person up and bustled them away.

Rising up, the wind funnelled through the window and headed towards Gabriel. He stood rock still, with his white cloak billowing behind him. Anything that moved in Isaac's bedroom slammed against the far wall. The wind continued to pour in and became hot. Isaac's bedside clock started to melt.

Gabriel opened his eyelids and turned to look at the scene. The devastation reflected over the curvature of his blue eyes. The fire, which had burned deep within him, rose with sulphur flames to the surface. As the rage approached his black pupils, they dilated to allow the flames an easy passage. Heat poured out of them and flickered over the surface of his eyes and as a fire danced around the reflected images, the room itself burst into flames.

Gabriel walked through the rising fire, stepped through the broken window and launched himself into the air. He rose; the sun throwing his shadow against the billowing black smoke.

The lost ones under Isaac's bed watched as the light from the fire pierced their dark world. One by one they got up and stood looking as the light approached them. The darkness shrieked in pain, sank below the carpet, and flowed down through a crack in the floorboards. The long years of despair lifted as a new hope dawned in their world. Each entered the flames and escaped through onto the other side.

A pile of Playboy magazines turned the flames blue as they burned, then the fire reared up from under the bed, swept past the fish tank and formed a fist at the bedroom door. Striking it with a jolt, the fury burst through; wood splintering the air. The four Clown Loach cooked, then shot into the room on waves of water tipped with fractured glass.

Surging around the upper floor, the fire reached the bathroom and flowed under the door to join the shroud of smoke covering the tiled floor. The flames picked up Isaac's electric shaver and flicked it on. The razor buzzed for a second, spluttered, and fell silent as it melted. Turning, the rage looked at the shower. Drops of water dripped from the showerhead. The sliding plastic doors cracked and flowed down into a sticky mess. The fire flickered up the tiled enclosure, surged through the nozzles of the showerhead and swept down through the tube into the pipes to melt the shower from the inside out.

When they had finished, the flames picked up the small specks left from the burning and cast them into the sky. As they rose, the fire played with them, shoving them to and fro in the billowing cloud. Eventually the specks rose too high for the flames to reach. Exhausted, they floated up on the up draft and peppered the clouds high up in the atmosphere. Stopping there to rest, they cooled in the cloud's embrace. Then gathering themselves, the remnants rained down onto a dying world.

Chapter 5
Who Shall Separate Us?

The sky rested over the landscape. Great swathes of deep blue sat cushioned on clouds that rolled around warm yellow sunflower fields. Standing before this summer scene stood a man dressed in a black assault suit. Wearing a respirator with large tinted lenses and a stubby black exhaust chamber, he paced up and down infront of the terminal adverts and spoke into his microphone, 'How many hostiles?'

'Four, Donaldson. We have half an hour before the deadline.'

'Do we know their positions?' said Donaldson.

'We have thermal image confirmation on three of them.'

'Do we have a clearance to go?'

'Waiting for the word. Stand by.'

Donaldson started his stopwatch on a thirty-minute countdown and took a deep breath through his mask's filter.

Ring, ring. Ring, ring. Ring, ring.

Donaldson looked across at his team.

'What the? Who's got their bloody mobile with them?'

His team motioned towards his back pocket.

'O,' he said. 'Forgot I had that with me. Excuse me.'

He pulled off his facemask, slipped his mobile out of his pocket and flipped it open.

'Yes?'

'Hello, Isaac.'

'Who is this?'

'It's Jane.'

'Who?'

'Jane Peter, we met last night.'

CLICK.

Donaldson hung up, switched off his phone and looked at his watch.

'GO. GO. GO.'

Donaldson's adrenaline kicked into overdrive and he surged forward with his two-man team. He ran along the wall advertising Morocco and stopped at the corner with his back pressed up against an advert with a slogan of *Hello Again!* The assault team leader from the red team on the other side of the mall, studied the thermal images in front of him, then looked across at Donaldson. His attention was distracted by Adriana Karembeu on the Wonderbra advert for a moment, then he signalled to Donaldson with his fingers. One hostile inside. Two civilians.

Donaldson broke cover. Running hard. Pistol in holder. Approaching target. Ten metres. Heart beat increasing. Adverts blurring. Eyes focused. Feet pounding. Eight metres. Arms punching back and forth. Breathing heavy. Time ticking. Five metres. Left hand up. Fingers spreading on stomach. Two metres. Stop. Right hand pulling out pistol. Cocking hammer. Squeezing trigger.

BLAM. He shot off the lock to the door. CRASH. His team kicked the door in. CLINK. CLINK. A flash bang stun grenade scampered along the floor. BANG. The noise billowed out into the room. FLASH. The magnesium flame flared.

'Go.' Left hand raised up in block. Right hand holding pistol close to chest. Inside. Turning face to right. Hostile located.

Donaldson pushed his right arm out towards the terrorist until his elbow locked into position. As he did so, he brought his left hand down and wrapped his fingers over his right hand. He dropped his left elbow to steady his shooting arm in a classic weaver grip. His two thumbs joined at the back of the Browning Double Action semi-automatic pistol, as he raised the weapon up and looked through the rear sight; he focused the front notch onto the hostile's chest cavity. Donaldson's lenses inside his eyes tensed causing them to bring the image streaming in through his pupils into a sharp focus. He braced himself and pulled back on the metal trigger. The skin on his finger went taut, losing its wrinkled texture.

BLAM. He braced his arms against the recoil, nudged his pistol down.

BLAM. The double tap sent a second bullet towards the target.

Donaldson raised the pistol higher and aimed again through its sights at the terrorist's forehead.

BLAM. The pistol kicked up, the nine-millimetre bullet raced off at two hundred and fifty three metres per second.

The spent bullet shell span up out of the gun to join the two shells hanging in the air. The striplight above the room shone down, glanced off the shell's hard metallic surfaces and streamed down to illuminate the scene below. The light reached out to the speeding bullet and etched a thin line along its length. The bullet accelerated with its new go faster stripe. The light pulled back up and threw three shell shadows flickering across Donaldson's outstretched arm.

The bullet clipped the edge of the terrorist's balaclava. The three shells fell to the ground and clinked against its hard surface; a soft thud filled the room as the man fell clutching his stomach.

Donaldson walked over, kicked him, and looked at the two civilians who had soiled themselves in the corner. He kicked the terrorist again.

Again, again …

The glint of gold on the finger of the man stopped him. Donaldson stared at the wedding ring then withdrew his knife and examined his reflection along the blade. Crouching down, he sliced off the ring finger.

The man screamed.

'What the hell are you doing?' said one of the civilians.

'Shut the fuck up, John,' said one of Donaldson's team at the door.

Dark blood pooled over the floor from the stub on the man's hand.

Donaldson aimed his pistol at the fallen man's head and squeezed.

BLAM.

The third member of the team looked around the door.

'Come on, time to go.'

Donaldson placed the severed finger in the metal bin on the wall.

'Come on.'

Donaldson's mobile started ringing again. He pulled it out, the screen was still dark. He placed it to his ear.

'Donaldson?'

'I'm coming for you, Isaac.'

'What the? Who are you?'

'Ha ha ha …'

CLICK.

Donaldson stood shaking for a moment. He reported back to control, 'Green team leader. One down. Two hostages secured. My position has been compromised. Shall I continue?'

'Proceed, Major.'

Donaldson checked his watch. Three minutes before the detonation. He listened as the blue team reported it had taken out two more.

'One left then,' he thought.

He changed magazines and stepped back out of the room into the airport shopping mall, his two men flanking him.

A music shop piped out last year's girlband smash hit. The music browsed through the deserted shops. It stopped for a moment above a coffee bar, then high on caffeine, gained altitude and floated up above Donaldson's head.

The mixture of coffee and music stirred him.

He looked around. A poster with a blue and yellow chequered strip running along the top of it, drew his gaze. It read …Have you seen this woman?

Name: Rebekah Steward

Year of Birth: 1977

Age: 27

Missing: March 2003

Sex: Female

Hair: Blonde

Donaldson looked up. The big clock suspended over the centre of the escalators showed three minutes to ten o'clock. His earpiece burst into life again, 'Satellite has picked up third hostile on the tarmac. He is on the move and carrying the bomb. Red team has located the other hostages.'

The voice paused. Then it continued with reverb distorting the flow of information, 'They've all been executed.'

'Shit,' Donaldson mouthed. Pulse racing he set off towards the departure lounge.

As he ran, the adverts strewn around the airport implored him to take a break ...

Get away from it all.
Relax by warm tropical seas surrounded by palm trees.
You owe it to yourself.

Donaldson checked his watch again as he exited the terminal. One minute left before the chemical bomb would kill all life within a twenty-mile radius of the city. Donaldson glanced at his Global Positioning System. The rest of his green team caught up and gathered around him. He pointed in the direction of a large airbus.

'Go.'

Donaldson ran hard. Rain spitting down. Surface slippery. Bullet-proof jacket heavy. Visibility poor. Information in his earpiece. Forty-five seconds left. Water spraying up under his feet. Location reached. Nobody. Running. Looking around. Wiping water away from visor. Nobody. Thirty-five seconds.

'Come on where are you?'

He stopped, looked around again, scanning for the target. Thirty seconds to go. Movement under an aircraft wing. A glint of light. He looked at the red dot of a laser sight from one of his team flickering around under the plane as it taxied down the runway. Faces peered out through the small windows dotted down the side of the fuselage. Donaldson's attention was drawn to a woman. She seemed to be searching for something in the rain. On seeing Donaldson she started beating against the window. Inside the cabin she screamed, 'Remember me.'

Donaldson struggled to place her, she looked familiar. A volley of bullets from under the plane's wing, broke his thoughts. They headed towards the SAS Hostage Rescue Unit.

BLAM. BLAM. BLAM.

Zing. Thwack. Thwack. Thwack. The bullets shattered the legs of the marksman next to Donaldson. The laser spot traced around the fuselage of the plane and shot up into the sky.

Donaldson dropped to his right knee. As he did, he bent his right leg around under him with a click and rotated his ankle to push his foot up onto its toes. At the same time, he pushed his left leg out in the direction of the shot and placed his left foot down with a splosh, onto the wet tarmac. In this secure triangular position, he drew his pistol from its holster.

His heart thumping inside him, he raised his weapon up with both hands and aimed it at the figure squatting under the wing. Drips of sweat poured from his forehead and trickled down the scar under his eye. Water droplets flowed down his polycarbonate lenses forming vertical stripes making it hard for him to focus. Ten seconds. He squeezed the trigger as another bullet from the terrorist nicked the side of his Kevlar Armour shield vest.

Zing. Thwack. Another slammed into one of his men, to the left of him who fell backwards his vest struggling to absorb the impact. As he hit the ground, water droplets sprayed up into the air creating a watery outline of the man. They hovered above him for a moment, before falling back again to rejoin the formless mass of rainwater.

'Fuck.'

ZING. A bullet went wide, and embedded itself into the luggage truck behind them.

Donaldson remembered the woman in the plane, he shot off another bullet.

BLAM.

It was the woman in the Police poster.

BLAM.

'She ...'

BLAM.

'...she ... is...'

BLAM.

A bullet punched a hole in the side of Donaldson's head. Blood sprayed into the rain. As he gasped his last lung full of dirty air, he watched the glow of the detonation billow out in the reflections on the runway.

Chapter 6
Pierced With Many Griefs

Isaac stared at the reflection of the billowing blossom cast in the sheen of water covering the road. Either side of him lines of banners flapped in the breeze. On his right flank they were blue. Those to his left were black and white. The flagposts supporting them spiked into the sky.

He ignored the fighting flags and passed under the trees. They stood silently, unconcerned at the battle lines proceeding their proud ranks. Underneath them black umbrellas bobbed along as if full stops punctuating the black suited commuters.

Isaac withdrew his gaze from the road and focused on the watery assault on his windscreen. The rain had grown harder and fatter and as each drop struck it flowed out from the shock to form a donut shaped ring.

'Who has been driving for the last five minutes?'

Isaac looked through the water donuts at the road ahead of him. The water writhed where the rain struck it, a multitude of tiny sprats floundering in the shallows.

Isaac's car cut two swathes through the sprats.

'How can I die in my own daydream?'

Isaac rubbed his forehead with his fingers locating a banging pain.

'Head shot, headache? No it was just a coincidence.'

He massaged his temple and started on his mantra to try to block the ache, 'Rebekah, Isaac, Jacob, Esau.'

The pain increased; it became difficult to focus on the road. The cars ahead of Isaac blurred around their edges; a buzzing sounded in his ears. He flicked on the wipers to clear the rivers of water flowing as if tears over the windscreen; the scene in front of him remained distorted. As he watched the colours of the cars changed.

The interior of his Porsche morphed into his old family saloon. The buzzing in his ears found their frequency and became the chatter of his five-year-old sons, Jacob and Esau, playing in the back. The beat coming from the car stereo increased as his music shifted up into Prodigy's 'Firestarter.'

'Heh, heh, heh,' went the music.

Isaac's heart rate increased to follow the tempo; he turned to look away from the road.

THUMP. THUMP. THUMP.

The soft eyes of his wife looked at him from the passenger seat.

Isaac's heart burned, tears started to well up. She laughed as her hair billowed in the wind. Isaac listened to her talk; her voice singing in the air. Raising her hand to her mouth, she blew him a kiss. Isaac reached out his hand to catch it, but it was gone, blown off with the wind to a place he couldn't reach.

Isaac looked up as the memory approached him. He had managed to keep himself from visualising the accident that shattered his life last year; now a great wave made of a myriad of images rolled up from the past and headed down the road.

A red car formed on the breaking crest of the wave. The car frothed at the edges and spat up millions of tiny yellow sand granules into the air around it. The wave deposited it onto the road in front of him with a thud, then broke, sending thousands of smaller images streaming towards him. A chocolate sponge cake bobbed up as the images started to sink into the asphalt. Isaac shook his head. The car before him started up. There was a sound of crunching gears, then a SPLAT as it drove over the cake. Splodges of butter icing flew up over the red car's windscreen; its wipers swept away the chocolate carnage. Isaac hit his brakes, no response. The approaching car increased its speed. Rebekah screamed.

Isaac heard the frightened voice of his sons behind him.

'Daddy, Daddy!'

Images sprayed up into the air from behind the wheels of the red car as they gripped onto the road. Among them Isaac saw champagne flutes spinning, cookies crumbling, intertwined daisies. The sound of 'Ocean Rain' by Echo and The Bunnymen, filled the air. Enhanced by the music, the emotional power of the memory sharpened. Rabbits bobbed up from the froth in response to the music and ran towards him. As they neared the safety of Isaac's family, two bright shafts of burning light shot out from behind them. The rabbits stopped and glanced back at the headlights. Isaac heard a thud thud thud, as the car mowed them down. Shielding his face from the white light, Isaac looked at the driver. He was dead, a thick noose around his neck. Over the noise of the wave Isaac heard distant singing ...

> Your face crumpled and tired is worn from the past,
> The hand of its memory smothers your laugh.
> Your smile weakens with each passing day,
> The light in your eyes is fading away.
> The strength you had was only an illusion,
> It fails you now, in your day of confusion.

For a moment there was silence. Then with a crash the car slammed into him. The front of Isaac's car crumpled towards him. The memory slowed, Isaac watched the faces of his family. He watched the smile of Rebekah being broken into a thousand pieces. He watched the light in his children's eyes flicker and die.

The memory faded. As it did, the airbag which had exploded into him withdrew back into the steering wheel, which morphed back into the wheel of his Porsche. The crumpled front of the car pushed itself out again and flowed back into the sleek curves of his sports car. The bodies of his family disappeared, the road ahead cleared, the slow beat of the music faded away. The car radio waded back into his mind with faltering notes.

Isaac sat alone again, top down on his convertible, listening to it. They were playing Blur's 'This is a Low.'

Isaac turned the radio off.

He stopped the car, got out and fell to his knees.

The rain slashed down onto his aching head. He knelt, holding his stomach and rocked back and forth.

Time passed by without helping. So did the multitude of people on their way to work, their white earpieces singing in the rain; a procession of random shuffles.

Drenched, Isaac slumped back into his Porsche and turned the key.

'If I can keep myself together,' he thought, 'I could be at the hospital in ten minutes.'

He wanted to sit and read to Jacob. Isaac often sat for hours chatting to him into the night; the doctors had said it was important to keep him stimulated. Once Jacob had slipped from his coma into a persistent vegetative state the doctors had become quiet. Isaac though continued to read, his words tethering his son to the land, a white knuckled grip that Isaac refused to release.

Chapter 7
A Deaf Ear to the Law

Time passed; the breeze snatched at the pink blossom above Isaac. The rain grew heavy and thick drops splashed down onto the tarmac sending out concentric ripples. As the rain hammered into the road the water rose up and picking up the swirling pink petals, carried them off.

Isaac sat in his car listening to the bird song above him. He closed his eyes and the morning chorus became the sound of distant singing. Lifting his hand, Isaac allowed a warble of pain to move from the back of his throat into the cold air. Images of golden leaves filled his mind; he stumbled forward towards the singing until he lost any sense of direction. Eventually the leaves cleared and he found himself in a vision of an open courtyard.

Isaac glanced around. Ancient olive trees, twisted around themselves as if in some inner struggle, grew up from a marble floor faced by an arc of stone seats. At its centre was a tree stump upon which sat a young boy, his head bowed. The child looked up as Isaac approached. Isaac stopped and stared into the cobalt blue eyes of his son.

'Esau is dead?' said Jacob.

Isaac reached forward, picked him up and held him.

Pain pushed against Isaac's ribs. The boy faded; a preacher rose up; the noise of singing filled the air from a congregation who appeared in the stone seats.

'Yes, you – you have a question,' said the preacher.

In the car, Isaac lowered his hands, 'No.'

'You had your hands raised.'

'I was holding my son,' said Isaac.

'This isn't school boy, if you have a question you only have to ask.'

'I…'

'The question boy, what is your question?'

'Am I dead?'

Isaac opened his eyes; wipers pushed the rainwater from his windscreen.

Water in the gully skidded over the drunken drains.

The tyres of a white car bore down on the streams of petals; the tread turned through the water and the car pulled over in front of Isaac's Porsche. Cherry trees, which had leaned in to whisper over Isaac, returned with a bounce to their upright stances; the birds perched on their outstretched arms flew up into the rain soaked sky. Lights flared up from the white car; it reversed and stopped.

A man got out. He looked at the open top of Isaac's car, the water trickling out from under the doors. Stuffing the last of a sandwich into his mouth, he walked over. White letters against a blue rectangle on the back of his padded jacket, identified him ...

POLICE

'Excuse me, sir, is everything okay?'

Isaac's thoughts tumbled from their precarious orbit and plunged into darkness.

'The question boy, what is your question?' asked the preacher in his mind.

'Are you hurt?' said his memory of a paramedic as he pushed the preacher aside.

Isaac looked at the inside of his sunglasses. In one lens stood the preacher; in the other the paramedic.

'What is your question?'

'Are you hurt?'

Isaac slid his sunglasses down his nose and peered over the dark lenses. For a moment he looked at the policeman, then the image blurred and he focused on the flowers in the rain.

'I have been involved in a horrific car crash,' he said finally to the policeman.

'Your car looks okay to me, sir.'

'Rebekah and Esau are dead.'

'I'm sorry to hear that,' said the policeman.

'Jacob needs the paramedic, where's he gone?'

'Look, sir, start from the beginning, what's happened to you?'

'I don't know.'

A Punch and Judy memory popped into Isaac's mind.

The five-year-old memory of Isaac appears, tears in his eyes. He is at the beach, lost and hungry; his Action Man hangs from his hand. Isaac looks at an ice cream van, wishing his daddy were there to buy him an ice-cream. A donkey thrusts hooves into hot sand behind the van. Where is my daddy to lift me up? The man holding the donkey looks right through Isaac. The smell of the fish and chips wafts across the crisping half-naked bodies lying behind him. Daddy I'm hungry.

Isaac shields his eyes from the glare and looks through the assortment of mix and match bodies. Holidaymakers mix with locals, flesh tans, children play, waves swim away as the tide recedes. Isaac threads his way past bobbing breasts and the blur of Bermuda shorts towards the red and white striped tent by the water's edge. It beckons him with its bright primary colours. Isaac sits with the other children. The start of the play is announced, with a blast from a trumpet; flaps are pulled away, the show begins. Punch appears. He has a large hooked nose, a humped back, a red and yellow costume. Under his long pointed chin sits a ruff; on top of his head bobbles the pointed tassel of a sugar loaf hat. Isaac watches. Judy appears in her mobcap and apron with their baby. Punch throws the baby into the crowd, Judy protests in her high pitched voice. The children laugh. Punch kills Judy, the family doctor arrives, Punch kills him too.

The children laugh.

A policeman is called. He scribbles the offence into his little black book. A terrible crime. Two speakers, sitting at the top corners of the tent, blare out ...

POLICEMAN   You must come down the station with me. You've killed your wife and child.

PUNCH   No! I'm going to take you down to hell.

Isaac laughs as Punch knocks the policeman down with his slapstick.

'That's the way to do it! That's the way to do it!' Punch sings out in a high pitched guttural voice.

Back in his car, Isaac continued to watch the rain falling in slow motion as shafts of sunlight picked out random droplets.

'Can I see your driving licence, sir?' the policeman said, pulling his fingers up and rocking them back and forth in a beckoning motion.

Isaac felt a desire to smash the policeman in the face.

'That's the way to do it! That's the way to do it!' sang out Punch from his memory.

Isaac fought down the voice, handed over his licence, and returned to the beach …

The wind picks up; red, white, and blue bunting flags flap as if trying to take flight. On stage, Punch goes on a killing spree with his girlfriend Pretty Polly. A blind man dies, as does a puppet called Scaramouche and his dog, Toby. The children laugh, their parents frown. Punch is brought to justice. Death, death, the sentence is death. The children hold their breath. The hangman, Jack Ketch, places the noose over Punch's neck and says, 'there'll be a hangin.' A younger child is dragged away screaming by his parents, 'I want to see, I want to see.' 'No you're not watching this ungodly show a minute longer.' Punch wriggles free and brings down his stick over Jack Ketch's head. The children laugh in relief, Ketch is dead. Death, death, the sentence is death. The Devil appears. Not even Punch can escape death. Death, death, the sentence is death. Pretty Polly holds up a card with Boo, written on it. 'Boo,' the children shout.

'That's the way to do it! That's the way to do it!' says Punch and kills the Devil himself. Pretty Polly cheers, they embrace and kiss. The curtain swishes back, small hands clap. Isaac laughs. In the laughter he forgets the fear of being alone.

After the show, his parents forgotten, he makes his way to the sea edge and splashes up and down, listening to the sounds of the ocean.

On the road, Isaac listened to the sound of the rain battering against the policeman's flak jacket.

'Mr Isaac Steward,' said the policeman, reading off the details. '30 Castle Street.'

'He killed death,' said Isaac, 'Punch and Polly will live together forever now.'

'Have you been drinking, sir?'

'I'm happy,' said Isaac, 'I can hear the ocean calling me.'

'Step out of the car please.'

Isaac turned on the ignition and switched the windscreen wipers on. The view ahead cleared and Isaac looked at the road as the Punch and Judy cast started to fall from the sky into the mirror of rainwater. The road blurred and became the ocean inside his mind …

Scaramouche splashes down into Isaac's subconscious; Toby gives out a yelp as he hits the water next to him. Scaramouche looks at his ruined embroidered waistcoat, 'This is an outrage, I am the legendary Scaramouche, a man of quality and debonair.'

He scoops up his long pointed hat floating next to him and places it onto his head. A stream of water pours down over his nose. Above him thousands of bubbles float against an ultramarine sky.

Judy splashes down, holding the baby and swims towards Scaramouche. Punch and Pretty Polly splash down, followed by the policeman.

Punch bobs to the surface and watches Pretty Polly push up out of the water in front of him. Her heavy dress pulls her down again. Punch swims towards her, unzips the back of her dress, freeing her from the weight of cotton and lace. Pretty Polly bobs up, laughs, unclips her peach bra and throws it at Punch. It hits him in the face. The policeman opens his little black book and writes: *Weapon: A peach satin brassiere, standard hook-and-eye metal clasps, 34 with coffee D cups.*

Punch removes Polly's bra with the end of his slapstick and looks at her; water slips off the waxy surface of her wooden breasts. Their swirling grain gleams; a sculpture oiled and buffed. The sea laps around her limewood nipples. Polly flicks her long wet hair over her right shoulder. The light catches the varnish in her pupils, putting a twinkle deep down within them. Punch grins. They disappear from view as the blind man lands, the red and white striped tent acting as his parachute falling over their wooden faces.

'Switch off the ignition and get out of the car,' repeated the policeman.

Isaac looked past him, images of Pretty Polly still in his mind.

'Mr Punch's girlfriend has got nice boobs.'

'What the hell did you just say?'

'The policeman is drawing a picture of Polly's boobs in his little black book,' said Isaac.

'Listen,' said the policeman, 'You think you can take the piss out of me? Get out of the bloody car.'

Reaching over, Isaac pulled down the handle on his door and swung it open. Chocolate wrappers flowed across the floor and spilled out of the car. The policeman looked down, as the rubbish fell over his shoes. Isaac slammed the door shut. As he did so, he felt the policeman's hand on his shoulder.

'I'm going to see my son,' said Isaac and shook himself free.

He slammed his car into reverse and screeched backwards. The policeman hesitated, then watched as Isaac sped away.

Isaac flicked on the radio to drown out the turmoil inside his head. His Porsche picked up speed. The Sargent cherry trees, with their dark red trunks, pulled back. Large industrial warehouses replaced them. Their reflections bore down onto the windscreen. With the back wheels leaving a cloud of spray behind, the car hit sixty miles per hour.

Seventy. Isaac entered a residential area. Telegraph poles lined the street. A sprawl of wires reached down to the houses from them dividing the sky above into slices. Their wooden limbs blurred into a line of exclamation marks, as the car shot under their webs and continued to accelerate. A speed sign flashed up seventy-six at him. Nothing registered in Isaac's mind. On the pavement a woman put a protective hand on her son's shoulder as he stepped off the kerb.

'Flippin' maniac.'

The car shrank into the distance.

Eighty. Traffic lights reached out with red fingers to stop him. Isaac brushed them aside.

The lone magpie, that had been following Isaac, flew over Iron Giants, which hummed with the electricity surging through their wires. Below, a man in a green oasis pushed his boy on a rusty swing; the boy kicking his feet at the sky. The magpie, squawked as Isaac's car threaded its way across town, a toy car on a game board. Through the beating rain the magpie dodged, floating ever upwards to keep Isaac in view. Finally it lost sight of the Porsche as a grey curtain of cloud swished down over it.

'What is your question?' said the preacher in the curve of black lens before Isaac.

Act 2
A Distance Between

Chapter 8
The Case of the Widow

A rip in the fabric under her chipped fingernails. A door ajar to her side. A window open before her; the linen of the curtains billowing. The leaves on the golden rain trees dancing on the wind. The iron gate contorted into form; an ornate barrier she cannot pass. The weight of death, pulling her back through the shifting gravel of the drive. She sits again; a rip in the fabric under her chipped fingernails.

Rebekah looked at the door to her side and waited again for Isaac to walk through in his slippers. Then she got to her feet, and holding back the curtains watched the golden rain trees dancing on the wind. Rebekah closed her eyes and pushed at the iron gate at the end of the drive.

'He could be standing at the door now,' she thought, 'he could be there, he could be...'

The attrition of doubt swept around her as the gates receded. She opened her eyes, turned to the door, then slumped back onto the chair.

Rebekah played again with the fabric under her fingernails and projected Isaac's smile, his eyes, his smell, into the gap at the doorway.

The iron gates swung open, leaving two channels arcing in the gravel. A car drove through, passed under the golden trees and pulled up in front of the house. Smooth hands rubbed a stubble-covered chin then tapped on top of the steering wheel. Dark eyebrows arched over narrow blue eyes. Ishmael turned his head, revealing the long straight profile of his Egyptian nose, and watched the long grass ripple around the house.

He looked up at the old roof, which resisted the crush of gravity trying to pull it and the white walls beneath into an archaeological dig. Instead, the past ate out from beneath the tiles into rough rendered walls, cutting windows into ancient stone. Drips of water fell down in front of his brother's window.

The wind blew, clouds parted, and the sun poured down onto the front of the house. Ishmael watched the beads of water lighting up, diamonds in the grass. The front door opened and Rebekah stepped out into the light. Ishmael got out of his azure blue Ferrari as she crunched up the drive towards him.

'Thank you for coming,' she said, as he offered a handshake. Rebekah ignored it, embraced him and kissed him on both cheeks.

'Let's walk together,' said Rebekah, 'I need to get out of the house.'

'Is my brother still here?'

'No, he left during the night. He is making the climb again today.'

Rebekah linked arms with Ishmael and the dead headed towards Mamre Wood. They walked in silence through Stubble Face Field, entered the wood and followed the path through the bluebells, their heads heavy from the days before. Golden brown leaves parted before Rebekah, blown up by the breeze. Twigs and bark snapped and twisted underfoot; mottled pale greens jostled above their heads. Before them, the land to their right dropped away into a deep depression in the ground. Shadows of trees reached out and painted stripes over the trunks lying there. Rebekah looked at the fallen giants as she passed and saw faces in their gnarled form.

A crystal river swept in from their left and ran parallel with the path. Rebekah and Ishmael stopped by it. Young shafts of greenery spiked up along the bank in between slumbering trees. Rebekah and Ishmael took off their shoes and dipped their toes in. Large stones ran across the river where they sat, marking off a boundary where the riverbed dropped. The water flowed over them and splashed down; bubbles skimmed over the surface.

'I want to pick some daffodils,' said Rebekah.

'Okay,' said Ishmael.

Rebekah turned to look at him.

'Thank you for walking with me.'

'That's all right,' said Ishmael.

They looked up as a kingfisher flew over the river towards them; its orange belly reflecting on the water below. It blurred into a streak of electric blue and dived. It resurfaced with a brown and black striped minnow between its dagger shaped beak. Returning to its perch, it smashed the flapping fish twice on the rock, then tipped its head back and swallowed it headfirst.

'Do you think he will make it?' said Rebekah.

Ishmael stared at his reflection in the water and kicked his feet. His image disappeared in the turmoil.

'It's been hard for you hasn't it?' said Rebekah.

'Yes.'

'I can listen, talk to me.'

'No,' said Ishmael, 'thanks but-'

'Please, Ishmael.'

'No.'

Rebekah put her hand into her pocket and took out Isaac's knife. She passed it over to Ishmael.

'I think he would have wanted you to have this.'

Ishmael looked at it.

'No ... I ...'

'Take it silly.'

Ishmael took the blade and plunged it into his pocket.

'Come on,' said Rebekah, 'you can cut the daffodils for me. '

They pulled their toes out of the water, slipped shoes over wet feet and walked on. Ishmael looked at the green moss obscuring the ringed memory of felled trees either side of them.

'Do you think that the dead forgive?' he said.

Rebekah stopped at the ring of sycamore trees, 'We're here.' She stared at the daffodils lying in the grass; they radiated out from the hummock as spokes of a great wheel. 'What's happened?'

'I remember this place,' said Ishmael. 'I used to play here. Where's the Dandelion Tree?'

'It blew down in a storm last year,' said Rebekah. She looked at the daffodils. 'Don't you think it's strange that they have all blown outwards?'

'Hmm? Yes, I suppose so. Look let me salvage what I can for you, and then let's get back to the house.'

Ishmael stepped into the ring. The wind stopped. The wood fell silent. Rebekah glanced around at the sound of footsteps behind her.

'Ishmael, can you hear somebody? Ishmael.'

Ishmael remained silent.

'Ishmael!'

Rebekah looked at him; he was staring at the spot near where the Dandelion Tree had stood. A distant rumble sounded below his feet; the earth bulged outward. The sound of footsteps increased and came from all directions, as if from a great army encircling them.

'Ishmael!'

Cracks appeared in the ground, water bubbled through, a mist descended, the sound of a roaring fire sounded out a death rattle from far below. Bright yellow smoke rose up through the cracks, the sky receded as a scroll, the yellow canvas billowed up shrouding the wood in darkness. Rebekah grabbed Ishmael's hand and pulled him from the circle. He stood before her, shivering.

'I'm so cold,' he said, 'so cold.'

Rebekah looked at the ground within the daffodils; a red glow deep below brought heat into the spring chill. Earth fell away, flames flickered and the unmistakable sound of horses snorting surrounded them. Rebekah could hear swords clashing around her, the sound of arrows taking to the air.

Ishmael fell to the ground and started to pray.

Rebekah started to scream.

Then all became quiet. Wind blew the yellow canvas northward, sunlight filled the clearing again, the fire withdrew. Birds began to sing. A sapling pushed up within the daffodils. Ishmael got to his feet and watched the green shoot push up into the air. Higher and higher it rose, and thicker and thicker it became, until a huge trunk soared up before them. Shade fell as branches grew. Emerald leaves sprouted filling the air with a sweet aroma. Fruit swelled up and tugged down on slender branches.

'Behold, the Dandelion Tree.'

Rebekah and Ishmael looked at Gabriel standing before them, a grey hooded cloak concealing his brilliance.

'Do not be afraid.'

'Who are you?' said Rebekah.

'Who I am is not important,' said Gabriel.

'What the hell just happened?' said Ishmael.

'There is no need for alarm, Ishmael, son of Abe.'

'How ... how do you know my name?' said Ishmael, 'Have we met?'

'No, now listen, you have been brought here for a purpose. You-'

Gabriel stopped and looked at Rebekah; she knelt by the Dandelion Tree crying. He walked to her, placed a hand on her shoulder, then knelt with her.

'What are you doing?' said Ishmael.

'Quiet now, Ishmael,' said Gabriel looking up. 'Let her mourn your brother.'

Rebekah nestled into Gabriel's arms and continued to cry. Ishmael stared at the large bag across Gabriel's back.

'What's in the sack?'

Gabriel got to his feet and faced Ishmael.

'Abe loved your mother; you need to forgive your father for sending you away. Forgive him; then you too can mourn.'

'What? Listen, he should have left Sarah for her,' said Ishmael.

'But, Ishmael,' said Rebekah, 'They were happily married, Abe loved her. Would you have it that Isaac didn't exist?'

'Yes,' said Ishmael, 'it all went wrong once he was born.'

'I understand your anger,' said Gabriel, 'that is why you need to forgive.'

Gabriel opened his sack and pulled out its contents.

'They're Isaac's,' said Rebekah as she saw the toothy grins of the crocodile ladder smiling up at her.

'Indeed,' said Gabriel. 'But they belong to Isaac's son now.' He looked at the crocodiles, laughed and spoke to them.

'Return.'

The ladder snaked through the grass and rose up into the tree. Gabriel turned to Ishmael and Rebekah, 'Now we climb.'

'You've got to be kidding me,' said Rebekah.

'Climb,' Gabriel repeated and started up the rungs.

Ishmael and Rebekah glanced at each other. Ishmael placed his foot on the first rung of the ladder. Rebekah watched him climb, then followed. They rose above the canopy of the wood and sat with Gabriel in the bowl formed by the branches. Rebekah looked at her house in the distance, Ishmael sat with his arms folded.

'Ishmael,' said Gabriel, 'you need to get Isaac to this tree before the sun sets tonight.'

'O please!' said Ishmael. 'Or?'

'He will be lost in the underworlds,' said Gabriel.

'Well post him a map,' said Ishmael. 'I hate him, he can rot in hell for all I care.'

'Many hands have been against you, Ishmael,' said Gabriel. 'Do you think it would be a good idea to free yourself of that curse?'

Ishmael looked away.

'Hmm,' said Gabriel, 'you need help.' He pointed skyward, 'Look.'

Rebekah and Ishmael looked upwards.

'So it's true,' mouthed Rebekah. She took a breath and allowed the reality of what she saw flood over her. As she did, she became aware of a tingling sensation in her toes; it rose up through her legs and flooded her body. She knew she could stop it whenever she wanted, but she was thirsty and let it rise until she felt her edges blur to join the blue around her and she became unsure as to where she finished and the sky began. She looked down as she ascended and saw the iron gate of her prison swing open. Leaves blew through from the golden rain trees. Rebekah felt her despair reach up to her from the ground with clenched fists, but she laughed and disappeared into the clouds.

Chapter 9
The Tempest Comes

Isaac climbed the stone steps leading up to the hospital. Behind him his car sat in the car park, its tyres smouldering in the rain. In his hands he held a plastic carrier bag containing a comb, paracetamol, a packet of cookies, a book, and his reading glasses. In his mind he held dominoes. Lots of them. He saw a line of them set out over the steps and into the hospital. As he climbed they fell before him and rippled through the door.

CLINK. CLINK. CLINK.

Isaac looked behind him and imagined fallen dominoes stretching back to the car. He stopped; looked around. Everywhere people walked with dominoes clinking before them.

'No,' he said, 'I'm not playing anymore.'

Isaac stepped sideways away from the line of black and white tiles.

'No.' He closed his eyes. 'I'm in a world where some God has set out a lifeline of dominoes before me. Forty years ago he flipped the first tile with my first cry. Off you go…

CLINK. CLINK. CLINK.

… out of the delivery suite to the fish bowl at the end of mummy's bed. An intricate pattern falling to produce a grand picture that can only be seen from far above. Falling, falling, always falling. Well,' Isaac took a deep breath, 'I will not fall. I refuse; I step away from the line. See …'

Isaac raised his fist into the air and looked up, 'See what I'm doing?'

SILENCE.

'You can take your clinkety clink and shove it.'

Isaac waited for the voice on high to boom, 'Get back in line.'

SILENCE.

'Right then,' said Isaac, 'right.' He straightened his tie and carried up the steps, leaving wet footprints behind him. At the lobby the line of dominoes turned right. Isaac turned left and took the stairs.

Puffing he climbed; at the sixth floor he stood for a moment to catch his breath then opened the doors onto the plastic coated corridor. The lift winked at him with its flashing arrow as he approached. Its doors opened with a swish and a line of black dominoes toppled from the back of the lift towards his feet. As the last started to fall, another tile appeared before it, then another, until the line stretched down the corridor. With a groan Isaac followed the tiles towards his son; pictures of clowns parading down the wall.

He stopped at the door to Jacob's room and closed his eyes.

'I need to get a hold of myself,' he thought as he remembered the face of the policeman looking at him. 'Keep it together.'

Isaac turned the handle and stepped through.

Jacob lay before him, small, helpless, damaged.

Isaac walked over and put his plastic bag down beside the bed.

'Hi, Jacob.'

Silence.

Isaac reached into his bag and took out the book, comb, his glasses.

'How are you? Shall we read?'

Jacob stared ahead; lost in a world he alone inhabited.

Isaac placed the book on the bedside table, straightened Jacob's bed covers and ran the comb through Jacob's matted hair. Isaac felt hair snag against the teeth.

'Sorry.'

When he had finished, he kissed the top of Jacob's head, picked the book up, and walked over to the window.

Outside the grass swayed in the breeze. Isaac looked up at the dark storm cloud building to the south. It threw a shadow over the land, draining the colour and lightness from the soil. Isaac watched it approach. He had lost the low on the way to hospital, now it had found him again.

He opened the book, put on his glasses, and started to read, 'Once there lived a fearful creature which had been ...'

As Isaac continued to read, his mind detached itself from the story and he thought of death. What will it feel like when my last domino falls? What happens when one by one my senses wither and die? Will I recede into my subconscious as my mind shuts down? Could I escape there or will that to cease to exist?

'... it roamed the land looking for knights to challenge ...'

Isaac looked at Jacob's dominoes spiralling in slow motion towards the metal frame of the bed. Waves of thick rain started washing down the windowpane. The air above the car park became cold. Isaac's face looked molten as if made of wax through the shifting water.

'... One day the creature discovered a knight on his knees praying under a tree ...'

With a roar, thunder swept over the assortment of cars on the tarmac, as if searching for one to taste.

'... and it devoured him. Inside the creature the knight remembered his bride. The creature died early the next morning, and the knight stepped out, blinking in the sunlight.'

Isaac paused from reading the book and pressed his hand against the window; darkness flowed around the base of the building. The old walls held for a moment, then, the weathered storm rose. Isaac flicked on the bedside light. Shafts of light shot around the bedside table and pierced the shroud that had fallen over Jacob. Isaac's eyelids fluttered and the soft sadness of loss drew teardrops as he remembered standing as Donaldson, looking at Rebekah in the plane.

'Rebekah... I ... I've forgotten you, I have never mourned you.'

Isaac turned and pulled the thin blue curtains across the window. He knelt before the grey plastic chair in the corner of the room.

Isaac's heart rate increased.

THUMP. THUMP. THUMP.

His headache followed the beat.

BANG. BANG. BANG.

The soft eyes of Rebekah looked at him from the passenger seat of his car. Isaac reached his hand out and brushed her hair away from her eyes. 'You provide the edges to my life,' he said. 'You shape the space around me. Without you I become all things, I become everything, I become nothing.'

Drops of water fell from Isaac's wet clothes and splashed around him.

Isaac heard the sound of Rebekah's breathing, he remembered the rise and fall of her chest, her chin resting on interlocked fingers and the sparks in the air around her which, when he touched one, made his toes tingle. He wrapped his love for her around these fragments. A bear rug from the hearth placed over goose pimpled shoulders. His heart thumped and shifted from its resting-place, moving outwards. A rumble sounded. The storm hovered for a moment high above the old hospital roof. Jacob's bedside light went out.

Darkness.

Chapter 10
Fair as the Moon

It was cold. Old trees jostled in the chilling wind; branches tipped with ice by their sides. Deep in the soil a residue of the summer warmed their twisted roots. The morning sun appeared over the horizon; bark groaned as the canopy swayed to and fro as the light looked for a gap in the wooden battlement. Ice encasing an old willow started to drip onto the ground. There was a crack and arthritic branches lifted; a low rumble tumbled over the landscape. Younger trees stirred at the noise, they yawned, stretching their limbs skywards, then went back to sleep. The light funnelled towards them. It brushed past their slumbering branches and streamed into the garden below.

The beams of sunlight pierced through the morning mist swirling around the lawn. At its centre, an ice-covered pond sat despondent in the chill. Snuggled down in the mud at the bottom, snoozed a family of tiny newts. They lay waiting for the touch of a warmer sun. The winter light stalled at this miniature moat, then skimmed over the sheen of ice like tiny flat pebbles.

Isaac's house stood before it, punching up through the mist. From the front, the house looked like a lighthouse in the middle of a misty sea. At the rear of the house, a narrow hallway window sent shafts of white arrows into the garden. High above sat a blue moon, still visible in the morning sky. It was full, yet pale against the bleakness of the December dawn.

The sunlight reached the base of the house and flowed around it looking for a way up. Finding some ivy, it rose over crumbling moss-covered brick and poured through the bathroom window. On the other side of the glass, the rays found a translucent blue mesh. They filtered through and lit the room in a pale blue hue. Standing in this haze was Rebekah. She stood with her cold feet on the tiled floor. Two gold bracelets wrapped around her slender right arm, a wedding ring around her finger, her nightshirt crumpled on the floor.

Rebekah studied herself in the bathroom mirror. She smiled at the picture across her pregnant stomach. It smiled back to her. She had awoken that morning to discover it - a large yellow smiley face painted across her bump, two black elliptical eyes above a broad grin. The pillow fight that followed had enfolded them in feathers and laughter.

'He's still just a big kid,' she thought, rubbing her stomach.

Washed in the soft light she looked radiant, her pregnant body glowing in its swollen form.

She turned and stepped into the shower. Reaching over, she span the temperature control to HOT and pushed the ON button. Her hair flowed around her shoulders as she looked up, preparing to wake under the water. A drip flowed out and rolled around the rim. It orbited the tiny holes peppering the showerhead, let go of the cold steel and fell towards her. The morning light caught it as it fell. It flickered through and cast blue light splashes across the tiles above Rebekah's head. The drip landed on Rebekah's freckled nose, trickled down her full lips and rolled down her neck.

'Come on,' she said. The words drifted out in front of her and condensed onto the shower door.

As if in response, another drip appeared. It dropped down onto her shoulder blades and slipped down her. It felt cold to the touch and Rebekah shivered; goose pimples covered her body. Rebekah bashed her fist against the chrome dial.

'Come on!'

Nothing.

Rebekah folded her arms over the top of her bump and rubbed them to and fro. Her thoughts tangled, snagged and tumbled from her; she took hold of them and fashioned swaddling to protect her unborn from her fears. She looked down at her freckles over her breasts to steady herself. On their first Christmas together, Isaac had noticed that the black spots traced out the constellation of the Little Bear. The freckle on her left shoulder was Polaris, the one on her right shoulder blade was Eta; the two

'Guardians' of the Little Bear, Pherkad and Kochab, lay just above her nipples. Little Bear had become Isaac's pet name for her.

Rebekah looked at her stomach pushing out from under her crossed arms.

There had been a time when she doubted she would fall pregnant.

Rebekah recalled the summer of 97; they had been trying without success for a baby for six months ...

Fade In:
Scene 1: Ext. Mamre Wood, Year: 1997 – Day   1

REBEKAH *and* ISAAC *sit under the shade of the Dandelion Tree. Around them are strawberries, a wicker picnic hamper, two half emptied flutes, a champagne bottle in a cooler box. They are both dressed casually.* ISAAC *wears a pair of ill fitting jeans and a red t-shirt. He looks scruffy, as if he didn't care.* REBEKAH *wears blue denim jeans, which sit below her oestrogen pinched waist. She has a sleeveless red and white striped top, worn under a cropped open jacket. The cotton of the top is pulled taut around her midriff by a knot tied in the material at the side of her waist. Lines of silk push out from her bra into the taut fabric; they curve upwards, the open pages of a paperback; a promise of hidden adventure with intimacy bringing connection, explanation. The straight cut of her top and the curve of her jeans frames her tummy below to form a tanned smile. Her belly button dips into the grin. A gold nose stud punches through her right nostril, the gold of her wedding ring glints in the light. Her lips, red, are open, her head tipped down. She raises her hand, brushes a wisp of hair from her face and starts to fiddle with her ear lobe.*

REBEKAH   I love it here.
ISAAC   This is where I used to come as a small boy, when I wanted to be alone.

REBEKAH *smiles, eats a strawberry, sips her flute of bubbles.*

ISAAC   I used to imagine being here with my girl. We'd kiss and share secrets together. It never happened of course.

REBEKAH   Until now.

ISAAC   Until now. (He kisses Rebekah) Tell me a secret then.

REBEKAH   Okay.

REBEKAH *pauses and looks up at the blue sky.*

REBEKAH   When I was seventeen …(she glances at Isaac) … we were poor, you must remember that.

ISAAC   Go on.

REBEKAH   Well I was out shopping with my girlfriend and we decided to buy our first Wonderbra. We wanted the *Hello, Boys* look.

ISAAC   Eva Herzigova

REBEKAH   Yes.

ISAAC   That advert had a profound effect on me.

REBEKAH   Well, that's one way of putting it.

ISAAC   No … well yes of course that, but it was those billboards that helped me decide to quit my casino job and get into advertising.

REBEKAH   What? Why?

ISAAC   It showed me the power of tapping into peoples' desires without warning on a large scale and I already knew how to do that on a smaller scale at the casino.

REBEKAH   Is this my secret, or an account of your meteoric rise in advertising?

ISAAC   Sorry, but … hang on, the first time I saw you –

REBEKAH   Yes?

ISAAC   I wouldn't have been there if I hadn't chosen to go into advertising.

REBEKAH   So?

ISAAC   Don't you see, Wonderbra brought us together.

REBEKAH   Well it brought Eva Herzigova's breasts together, I'm not sure if you can credit it for us.

ISAAC   Hurrah for Wonderbra!

REBEKAH   (laughs) Shut up, Isaac. My story, remember? Well the problem was we had no money.

ISAAC   You stole a Wonderbra?

REBEKAH   Er ... yes, you are the first person I've ever told, I felt guilty for months.

ISAAC   Did you have it on the night we first saw each other?

REBEKAH   (sighs) Yes.

ISAAC   There you are, fate at work.

REBEKAH   (raising her eyes) Enough. Go on, your turn, tell me a secret.

ISAAC   When I was five, I climbed this tree for the first time. When I got to the top I saw people flying above me.

REBEKAH   And you since discovered the marvel of aeroplanes?

ISAAC   No, Rebekah, they were flying. It was like I was dreaming and flying with them. They gave me chocolate and sang to me.

REBEKAH   Isaac, that is a memory formed by the overactive imagination of a small boy.

ISAAC   Is it?

REBEKAH   Is it? Of course it is ... are you serious?

ISAAC   Yes.

REBEKAH   Okay, why don't you climb the tree and show them to me?

ISAAC   You won't see anything. Not if you don't believe.

REBEKAH   I think it will help.

ISAAC   (sighs) Okay, come on then.

REBEKAH *and* ISAAC *climb the crocodile ladder. They both look up and see nothing. They climb down.* REBEKAH *looks at* ISAAC.

80

REBEKAH   I guess that's two of us that don't believe then.

ISAAC *looks at her. A north wind starts to blow. It is joined by a cool wind from the south. Rain starts falling. The first drops hit the side of their champagne flutes, which reply by ringing out with accompanying pings. The drops roll down the mouths of the crystal and disappear into the liquid. The rain grows heavy. It smashes into their picnic and flows over them. The sweet fragrance of wet grass floats up. REBEKAH and ISAAC stand in the rain and fight the instinct to flee. REBEKAH reaches out and runs her finger down the scar under ISAAC'S eye. She looks at him for a moment, her eyes shimmering. They pull into each other and kiss.*

ISAAC   Stuff the rain, let's just get wet.

REBEKAH *nods. ISAAC pulls off her jacket and reaches down to undo the knot in her T-shirt. He pulls it off over her head and unclips the metal hooks in her satin bra.*

ISAAC   Not your Wonderbra.
REBEKAH   It's in the wash.

REBEKAH'S *nipples are erect, towers against the battering of the tiny raindrops. She looks into ISAAC'S glistening eyes. Her knickers are blue; there is a stitched pattern of a love heart in a red square centred on their band. REBEKAH puckers down the heart: she is clean shaven. ISAAC pulls his wet clothes off. REBEKAH looks at him and laughs. He has shaved his chest. ISAAC and REBEKAH clasp hands together. The rain paints a sheen of water over REBEKAH in soft fluid brush strokes. It disrupts the play of light and shadow over her body giving her an element of abstraction in her form. The result is a picture of a lover clothed with a nudity conveying innocence, confidence and purity hinting at divinity. The lovers wriggle their wet toes and start to move from under the*

81

Dandelion Tree. They feel no shame in their nakedness as they run laughing through the thick grass. A low murmur rolls out from the trees, as they witness a sight unseen since the beginning of all things. ISAAC and REBEKAH catch each other under a pear tree. They wrestle and fall to the ground.

End of scene.

Rebekah smiled as the memory faded. The shower continued to drip down across her star system. One of the drops flowed over Pherkad. The image of the star distorted in the curvature of the water droplet as it passed by on its voyage. The drop fell from the underside of Rebekah's breast, rolled around her swollen stomach and passed through one of the eyes of the happy face. Picking up some paint, it smeared a black line over the bright yellow background forming a black tear under the eye.

The shower started; water drummed down onto the cubicle floor.

Rebekah's tummy jutted out of the flow, which streamed around her bump. She thought about her boys growing inside her, 'I wonder what your aspirations will be? Your hopes and dreams? What will you become? Who will you fall in love with?'

As she pondered over the thousands of uncertainties to come, she remembered the feeling of certainty she had experienced five months ago …

Fade In.
Scene 2: Int. Hotel Apartment, Year: 1997 – Day   2

REBEKAH *stands in the shower. A tiny white moon is tattooed onto her darkened skin where her right hip flows into her stomach. The water stops, plastic doors open over the moon.* REBEKAH *steps out. She dries herself and wraps her towel around her hips.* REBEKAH *walks into the bedroom and sits to brush her hair.* ISAAC *is on a king-sized bed. He wears a pair of green Bermuda shorts, which clash with his eyes. He looks up at her back and watches the outside curve of* REBEKAH'S *breast move at her motion like the bob of a buoy pushing outward at the bow of a boat.*

ISAAC   Look at this; we could have fresh lobster sent to our room!
REBEKAH   Not for breakfast, Isaac.
ISAAC   And champagne, we could get drunk on champagne!
REBEKAH   (sighs) Isaac, can we ask again?
ISAAC   I'm tired of asking.

ISAAC *looks up from the menu and looks at* REBEKAH.

REBEKAH   Humour me one last time.

ISAAC *gets up and walks over to* REBEKAH. *He sits next to her, takes her hand. He stares straight ahead at the reflection of* REBEKAH *naked in the mirror, prays and asks for a child.*

End of scene.

Scene 3: Ext. Beach, Year: 1997 – Night   3

ISAAC *and* REBEKAH *walk down the beach towards the sea.* REBEKAH'S *arm wraps around* ISAAC. *She leans into her lover as they walk. The light of the full moon falls across them. The ties to* REBEKAH'S *bikini flutter behind her back. Two bows and two thin strips of sun washed blue unravel and fall away to join the daises on* ISAAC'S *Bermuda shorts. They wade through the sea and stand in the waves.* ISAAC *reaches out and runs the back of his fingertips over* REBEKAH'S *cheek.* REBEKAH *arches her back and raises her hands; her breasts push forward, her bottom curves outward and she seems to summon the waves towards her; they roll up over her head, dancing horses that pound down around them in bubbly froth. Laughter rises up into the night sky. They embrace.*

The sea rises in waves, warm, relentless; semen rises, warm, urgent.
They wade back. Bubbles from the waves spin up around their feet.

REBEKAH   We've just made a baby haven't we?
ISAAC   You have that feeling too? Yes. Yes, I think
the answer is yes.

Fade out.

Rebekah smiled. They had hugged each other when the doctor had told them she was pregnant.

'Soon we shall be a family,' she thought. 'Is the world ready for Isaac as a dad? Am I ready?'

Rebekah stepped forward and let the water flow over her hair. She reached for a bright blue shampoo bottle and flipped open its lid with a POP. Squeezing a gloop of liquid into the cup of her hand, she closed her eyelids, shutting out the blue of the room. Rebekah breathed in the scent of the ylang ylang tree, which floated around her in the hot steam as she massaged the shampoo into her hair. The mirror above the sink misted over. Without the reflections, the room shrank and became intimate.

Rebekah smiled as she rubbed her fingers into her scalp. She replayed the events from the night before in her mind …

Fade In:
Scene 4: Int. Bedroom, Year: 1997 – Night   4

ISAAC *and* REBEKAH *are in bed. It is one am.* ISAAC *is asleep. He breathes in silently through his open mouth, then out gently through his nose; it sounds as if he is deflating. The bed sheet holds him from falling out of bed, a trawler net straining to hold the days catch.* REBEKAH *sits reading. The meaning of the words glances off her tired eyes. She places the book down, switches off the light and tugs the sheet from* ISAAC. *Hours later she is still awake. The stillness of the night picks at her consciousness, fingers that play yet never remove the old scab. Passing cars scan beams of light around the ceiling, the hands of a clock marking time.* REBEKAH *finishes packing her troubles into the removal van parked up on the outskirts of her mind. Exhausted she waves it on ahead of her into the morning and looks across at* ISAAC.

REBEKAH   I love you.

Her words float down over him and touch him, the coming of a summer breeze. ISAAC *stirs as the words soak into him and* REBEKAH *knows that inside they find resonance.*

REBEKAH   We are complete, we are one.

REBEKAH *closes her eyes; her eyelids flutter as she starts to dream. The sound of rain beats against the bedroom windowpanes. A gust of wind blows them open. Leaves blow in and settle over their bed.* ISAAC'S *eyelids start to flutter. He opens his eyes.*

ISAAC   Why have you left me, Rebekah?

ISAAC'S *face sets into a grimace and goes a shade of blue. He sits up.*

REBEKAH   Isaac, I'm here.

ISAAC *doesn't reply. He sticks out his right arm and looks straight ahead.*

REBEKAH   Are you awake?

ISAAC'S *right index finger twitches. He falls back onto his pillow with a thud.* REBEKAH *nudges him to see if he really is asleep.*

REBEKAH   Isaac, please come back to me.

REBEKAH *lies back, stares at the flaking paint on the ceiling, continues to dream.*

Fade out.

Rebekah tipped her head back. Thousands of bubbles streamed over her as the shampoo rinsed from her hair. They traced over her shoulders, slipped down her back and swept down her long legs onto the floor. There they span around her toes and disappeared in a swirl down the plughole. Raising her hands, Rebekah wiped the water from her face and opened her eyelids. Now awake fully, a light shone from her deep blue eyes.

With her hair fresh and revived from its slumber, Rebekah stepped back into the flow of the shower. Rivers of hot water poured down. A tiny stream broke away and trickled across to the tear on the happy face. The water picked up the paint from the smear and carried away the tear. Rebekah rubbed her sponge over the picture and it disappeared in a streak of yellow and black.

Bending her knees, Rebekah lowered herself onto the shower floor. Reaching forward, she picked up a can of shaving mousse and squelched out a ball of foam into her palm. She rubbed it over one of her legs, sprayed out some more foam and lathered up her other leg, until her legs were iced. Taking her razor, she started removing the festive foam in strips; her bump making it difficult. She finished, stood up and let the water wash over her smooth legs.

As Rebekah prepared to step out, she felt a thump in her stomach. Another followed. She looked down at her tummy.

'Isaac, quick, get in here!'

The bedroom door opened. Rebekah listened, above the patter of the shower, as Isaac's footsteps padded down the hall. She glanced up as he peered around the door.

'Er ... yes?' he said, looking at where the happy face had been.

'They're kicking.'

Isaac stepped into the room and opened one of the shower doors. He placed a cold hand on her glistening tummy.

Thump.

A pause.

Thump thump came the reply.

'See what you mean,' said Isaac. 'We'll have our hands full with these two.'

Isaac smoothed his hand over her stomach.

'You look amazing; I love you looking like this.'

She smiled as she watched a twinkle form in the depth of Isaac's eyes. Rebekah's eyes responded. They opened wider and the light within shone.

Isaac slid open the other door, stepped into the shower, and pulled Rebekah towards him. She raised her hands and put them around his neck.

The two lovers entwined. Spray hatched down and covered them in a watery veil. Drops span off and tapped against the plastic of the shower doors. Isaac pushed the wet strands of hair away from Rebekah's face, kissed her, touched her breasts.

Rebekah's body, flush with hormones from the pregnancy, responded; their lips melted like chocolate into one another, their toes left the dimpled surface of the shower tray and they drifted up through the water. Rebekah's nipples rose as they passed up through the white ceiling. Isaac's cock rose as they sailed through the wooden cross beams. Another kiss pushed them through the brittle slate of the roof. Isaac hooked his foot onto the aerial sitting on top of the chimneystack. They stopped, tethered. A banner to their house swaying rhythmically in the mist; their naked bodies turned blue in the December air.

The shower tugged at them as they bobbed together. It spluttered and went icy cold. The effect like the fumble of small fingers at the door.

Isaac and Rebekah hit the floor with a BUMP!

Isaac reached over and thumped the OFF button. The shower continued to pour cold water over them. Rebekah and

Isaac threw themselves out of the shower and stood shivering before each other.

'Stupid, stupid piece of junk,' said Isaac. He grabbed his towel and started to dry himself.

'When are we going to get that fixed?' said Rebekah.

'Fixed? I'm going to dismantle it bit by bit and grind it down.'

He reached over, tugged at a towel hanging over the radiator and threw it towards Rebekah.

'Throwing in the towel?' she said as she wrapped it around her and let its warmth seep in.

'Very funny. I think our cold shower has killed the moment don't you?'

Rebekah looked at him, took a step forward and released her grip on her towel. Placing her hands around his neck, she wrapped herself around him. She kissed his surprised face and little by little nudged him back towards the shower. Then with a gentle shove she pushed him away. Unable to stop himself, Isaac stepped back into the cold water. Rebekah shut the shower doors and held them closed.

'Ahh,' cried Isaac as the cold water flowed over him. He thrashed his arms and battered the shower doors with his fists.

'Let me out! Let me out!'

Rebekah held the doors closed as Isaac clawed at it with his fingers.

'Face paints are for kid's parties,' she said. 'Not your wife's pregnant stomach.'

Isaac reached for the showerhead to try to turn it away. It was stuck. He gave in and looked up at his watery nemesis as a chill started lapping over his feet. He curled his toes upwards, spat the water out from his mouth and glared at Rebekah.

'Okay, okay,' he said, 'you got your revenge. I'm sorry. Now let me out, this thing is trying to drown me.'

Rebekah kissed him through the plastic, flicked her foot and kicked his towel into the corner of the bathroom.

Isaac placed his hand up against the shower doors. The pads at the ends of his fingers formed white islands in the stream of water running down the inside.

'Rebekah, please let me out.'

He softened his big blue eyes and looked at her. Rebekah placed her hand against his on the other side of the plastic, then reaching over she released the doors. Isaac opened it and stepped out. He stood shivering, soaked in the freezing water.

'M … m … my head is freezing. I … I … think I started hallucinating in there.'

'Don't be silly, Isaac.'

'No, for a moment you seemed to recede into the distance. I heard voices.'

'I love you, Isaac.'

Rebekah rubbed Isaac's wet hair with her towel and kissed him.

'Come on,' she said and took his hand.

They stepped out of the blue glow of the sunlit bathroom into the hallway. Isaac's body, invigorated from the cold, tingled as if drops of snow were falling onto his skin. A tear formed in Rebekah's eye, she gathered herself, walked through a pile of green leaves carpeting the landing floor and entered the bedroom.

A table lamp, sitting on Rebekah's dressing table, lit the room. Isaac bent down, swept the House Beautiful magazines from the bed onto the floor and fell onto the mattress. Feathers from the split pillow billowed into the air. Rebekah set herself on top of Isaac then pushed herself up on her hands. She blew at a feather floating down between them and shifted her weight onto her fingers. Her shadow on the vanilla wall became hard and defined, as if the light had bounced off curves of marble to mark her nakedness for prosperity.

'You first.'

'Okay,' said Isaac. He fell silent for a moment, then said, 'Your kisses are like tasting sweet honey.'

Rebekah smoothed a hand over one of his arms.

'Your arms are like the trunks of the great oaks of Mamre, steady and firm.'

Isaac tickled the underside of her feet with his toes.

'Your breath is like the freshness of a summers breeze.'

Rebekah shook her hair over him, showering him in water droplets. With her right hand she swept some of her hair back over her head, 'Your words are like the blowing of the north wind, billowing the canvas of my spice laden ship, drawing me safely to your shore.'

Isaac wiped the water from his face, wrapped his hands around her neck, and pulled her face down towards him. Kissing her nose, he said, 'Your face is as fair as the moon. The sparkle in your eyes is like the glistening of the morning dew.'

Rebekah kissed him. He felt warm against her skin. Isaac reached up, kissed her breasts and brushed his erection against the side of her clitoris; white clouds billowed through Rebekah's mind.

'Your leaving is like the shedding of leaves in the autumn,' said Rebekah, tears glistened in her eyes. 'Your return warms me like the first touch of summer on a frost laden garden.'

Isaac grasped the strands of wet hair in front of him.

'Your fair hair is like the grasslands of Moriah. Your breasts are like two lion cubs that hide there, waiting to pounce from their cover.'

Rebekah smiled and jiggled her breasts.

'I'm torn,' said Isaac, 'between looking at your bouncing boobs and your beaming face.'

'Multi-task.'

'Very funny.'

Rebekah ran her finger over the scar under Isaac's face.

'Your face is like the rocks of Horeb,' she said, 'It holds stories chiselled by the north wind.' Rebekah looked away and said, 'Give in?'

'No ... your eyes are like sparkling blue sapphires, washed in milk and set into the tumbling streams that refresh the grasslands of Moriah.'

'Disqualified,' said Rebekah. She reached down and wrapped her fingers around Isaac's erection.

Isaac raised an eyebrow.

'You used the grasslands of Moriah already,' she said. 'So I win.'

'You sure you don't just make up these rules so you'll win. Who says I can't mention the same thing twice? Where's the rule-'

Rebekah pulled Isaac's cock up into the air; engaging a brake, it stopped Isaac's flow of words. Rebekah lowered herself down onto him.

Summer entered the cold winter room as they found their rhythm. The ceiling to the bedroom rolled away and their music rose up punching holes into the mist. They floated off the bed. Isaac came and, as if severing a tether, fell back to the bed with a thud. He lay there looking at Rebekah's naked body drift off into the sky, her hair strewn out around her as if adrift in the depths of water. Her eyes, dreamy and intimate, met his across the distance between.

Seeing her, a flock of ravens burst from the thicket behind the row of sleeping trees. The black mass soared upwards across the disc of the rising sun, banked northwards and flew across Rebekah. For a moment Isaac imagined he saw a gun held by a strip of tape across Rebekah's back, but then black wings brushed down and hid her from sight.

Chapter 11
Among the Trees

The sun appeared as the clouds parted, a hidden lover bursting from wardrobe doors in glory. Shafts of yellow streamed towards the blue land. The touch tender, began to dry up the pools of rain across the pavement. A yellow-brown house spider appeared from under a rock; it scuttled across to a gutter running down the edge of a large building and started to climb. It stopped at a window and inspected the remains of its web strung out across it.

Isaac pulled back the curtains and blinked in the sunlight. As his pupils contracted, he could see the pale moon in the rain rinsed sky. The movement of the spider before him caught his eye and he focused on the small web. Drops of rainwater hung on the intricate strands. One drop fell from its sticky embrace and fell across Isaac's blurred image of the moon behind it.

A scattering of crows flew up from the trees in the courtyard. They banked across the moon and headed straight for the window. Isaac stood back and placed his hand across his face to protect himself. Pulling back their black wings they slowed, then swooped over the building. Isaac watched them as the memory of Rebekah from six years ago was carried by the birds back to the prison in his mind that was Temporal Gyrus.

Remembering Rebekah had been like a bomb detonating and the sum of her blew his mind apart. Shock waves rippled through him, knocking his thoughts from their course, the blast throwing memories through membranes; all her energy surging towards him and into him. It felt as if he had soaked up the entire force of her within. That he was a sink to her. And then. Then he had to stand and hold it all in. Hold her and remember her. And he felt at any moment he would fail, the pain would succeed and he would burst into a blaze of dust into the sky.

'Why have you left me, Rebekah?'

'*Isaac, I'm here.*'

Isaac opened his eyes and looked around the room.

'*Isaac, please come back to me.*'

Isaac reached up and ran his fingers through his wet hair. Water from his sodden clothes continued to drip onto the floor swelling the gathering puddle.

'I'm going mad.'

Knock knock.

'Yes?' said Isaac.

A nurse walked in.

'Mr Steward! What happened to you?'

'I got wet.'

'You planning to stay as usual?'

'Yes.'

'Not very talkative today?' said the nurse as she plugged a heart monitor sensor onto Jacob's finger.

Isaac shook his head.

'Wait a moment.'

She left; a few minutes passed, then she reappeared with a hospital gown and a polystyrene cup full of steaming coffee.

'Stick this on. I'll see these get dried for you,' she said, tossing the green gown over to him.

'Thanks.'

Isaac looked at her name badge pinned to her chest. It shimmered and changed from Deborah to Rebekah, then disappeared along with the rest of her uniform. Deborah smiled, set the coffee down, and turned her back to him.

Isaac pulled off his shirt and trousers, his mind full of echoes of Rebekah naked in the shower. For the first time since the road kill, Isaac's cock twitched. A resurrected rabbit, it rose as blood flowed.

Deborah glanced in the mirror beside her as steam from the coffee misted over it. Isaac noticed her eyes linger at his reflection. He looked at himself in the image; the rabbit had hopped out into the middle of the road and stood blinking in the light.

'O shit, I'm sorry.'

'Don't worry.'

Deborah turned and taking the starched hospital gown slipped it over him. Isaac nervous at her proximity, fumbled at the ties behind his back.

As he did, he mentally dressed her again, but he tingled at her touch and the smell of her flowed up his nostrils sending signals that kept him erect. She smiled again, 'Turn around.'

Isaac conceded defeat to the cotton ties and turned away, his hands between his legs. Large black letters stamped on the back of the gown warned, HOSPITAL PROPERTY. Deborah tied a bow, then scooping up his wet clothes, walked to the door.

'Thanks,' said Isaac.

She smiled and left.

With the smell of Deborah still in his nostrils, he tried to focus on Rebekah again. Thoughts tumbled around him like lottery balls flung into motion. Every few moments one rolled out to find its place in the sequence.

He sat down and placed his head in his hands.

Darkness.

'*Isaac, please come back to me.*'

'*Isaac, please come back to me.*'

'Think about Rebekah,' he said into the darkness, 'think about Rebekah.'

Laban staggered out of the Subconscious Tavern and looked around.

'*Think about Rebekah.*'

'Rebekah?' thought Laban. The thought fragmented in the swill of Memento Melt flowing through him. 'Now, which way is home?'

The table that had floated out of the tavern in the early hours of the morning moved across the doorway and barged into him.

'Get lost,' said Laban, 'Stupid table.'

The table bumped into him again.

'Look beat it,' said Laban, his head spinning.

THUMP.

94

Laban fell unconscious onto the table's beer stained top. The table floated for a moment, then drifted off down a passage carrying its sleeping rider.

'Think about Rebekah.'

Laban woke with a jolt. He looked up and stared at a portal entwined with willow. It grew to fill his vision, then shrank again. Laban floated up from the table as it continued to knock repeatedly into the portal.

'Down, stop it,' he said to the table.

He looked at the portal again. The table span around and bumped Laban towards it.

'Is it in there?'

Laban fumbled in his pocket and struggled to focus through the clear membrane into the light beyond.

'I can't find my keys.'

Laban pushed his hand through the portal, then withdrew it again. Sticky fluid from the membrane stuck to his fingertips and the portal bowed out towards him following the movement of his hand. Laban swam back and lit a cigarette.

'Right.'

Laban pushed the cigarette against the portal; a small opening appeared around the tip. Laban blew on it until the hole became larger, then staggered through. The membrane snapped back into place behind him, wobbled then settled into its smooth convex shape. Globules of fluid shot out from it as it spat out the fowl taste of Laban.

Laban glanced around, 'This isn't my house. Where's my bed?'

Laban looked at the trees lining one side of a narrow path that stretched away into the distance. Their trunks threw dark shadows onto the lane. The sound of running water from a clear river on the other side of the path soothed Laban's aching head.

Hearing a rustling noise, he turned; one of the coils of willow was unwinding from the portal. The strand dropped down

95

onto the floor and morphed into a snake. Laban watched it slither towards him.

'Um ...' he said, the alcohol dividing the snake into two and changing it into two scantily dressed woman, 'Hello girls. Do you like jokes? - I can tell a good joke.'

The snake hesitated. Laban lurched, then straightened out.

'Once upon a time,' he began ...

There lived ... there lived ... a snake. Yep that's it, a snake. And the snake lived in a lush garden, with trees bearing all different kind of fruit that were good to eat. God had told the snake it could eat any of the fruit on them apart from the fruit of one tree. The tree of life. One day a woman and a man walked past the snake and looked down on it.

'Sod off,' said the snake. 'These are my apples.'

'O my,' said the woman. 'A talking snake.'

The man looked at the snake in surprise.

'Are you sure?' he said. The snake looked at him.

'Yes. It spoke to me,' said the woman. 'Go on snake, say something else.'

The snake hissed.

'Hmm,' said the woman. 'Stupid animal.' She bit into an apple from the tree and then stuffed it into the snake's mouth.

'Arh, I'm naked,' shouted the snake, as it swallowed the apple whole.

'You're right,' said the man biting into another apple. 'A talking snake ... wow.'

The snake slithered away and hid in some fig leaves under the tree.

'Er ...' said the woman, folding an arm across her boobs, and placing a hand between her legs, 'Do you think I'd better cover up, someone might be watching us.'

'Dunno,' replied the man lowering his hands and looking around. 'I suppose. Does that involve shopping?"

Laban looked at the boob tubes before him.

'Funny isn't it?' said Laban. 'Would you like a drink?'

The snake hissed and continued to slither towards him.

'Great,' said Laban and collapsed onto the floor.

The snake flickered its forked tongue and circled him.

A small bird swooped down from a hollow in a tree above. Tucking in its spotted, grey-blue wings, it grabbed the back of the snake's head and flew over the river with the snake thrashing in its bill. It hovered for a moment, then snapped shut its black bill.

The beheaded snake dropped towards the tumbling water. Its body hit first, sending up a line of droplets into the air. The head hit a moment later and sent a fat droplet up to join the watery line, punctuating the air in an exclamation. The snake thrashed its red and black body as the river engulfed it. Venom spat up from the head towards the bird. Caught in a strong eddy of water, the snake slipped under the surface and disappeared. The bird gave out a great rolling laugh and returned to a branch.

Laban got to his feet and stood motionless for a moment looking at the river. As he watched, the red and black skin of the snake floated up to the surface. Laban shook his head, backed away and staggered along the lane, his shoes crunching on the debris of twigs and dry leaves.

As Laban walked, the wonder of the world around him lifted his gaze and his head started to clear. Looking around, he realised the trees moved with the seasons along the lane. Those next to him wore golden autumn coats, farther down the lane he saw winter trees their branches low with the weight of snow, beyond them the blossom of spring. A gentle breeze whispered through the autumn canopy. It picked up their leaves and golden rain fell onto the lane around Laban. He watched them spin around at the edge of the water, then lifting his hands, he let the autumn shower flow through his fingers. Dancing, he carried on along the lane, catching leaves and stuffing them into his pockets.

Laban slowed as he left the autumn section and the breeze dropped. Shivering he looked down onto the path as he passed the winter trees. As he focused, his eyes became accustomed to the bands of shadows on the path. He stopped at one of the shadows. Deep within the blackness he saw bubbles moving. He watched as they span in and out of each other.

'Laban, what are you doing here?'

Laban turned, 'I … I … Uncle, is this Bethuel's Leap?'

'Yes.'

'It's beautiful.'

'Laban,' said Jidlaph, 'Isaac has managed to pull Rebekah from Gyrus, but she has been taken and I fear that he will not succeed again.'

'Do you still believe she will return?'

'Yes, Laban, look around you.'

Jidlaph swung his arm out and swept it around Bethuel's Leap.

'This is a place of love and death. Isaac and Rebekah first spoke to each other here and here your father leapt to his death trying to escape the custodians.'

Jidlaph placed his hand on Laban's shoulder, 'One day we will avenge him, Laban, perhaps even this day, there is still hope.'

'Why are you here, Uncle?' said Laban, 'Shouldn't you be at Gyrus helping Rebekah?'

'I can help her here, Laban. I've spent the last year copying Isaac's key memories of Rebekah from Temporal Gyrus and inserting them as memories into Isaac's memory of Bethuel's Leap.'

'O my God!' said Laban, 'The custodians will kill you.'

'They don't know. Now look up.'

Laban craned his head. For the first time he noticed coloured balloons floating above the canopy.

'Wow.'

'Unfortunately the memories are unstable,' said Jidlaph. 'They are only impressions of the real thing.'

'You can get them into Isaac's mind?'

'Yes, the shadows you see cast down by the trees onto the path project the image directly into Isaac's mind.'

'What?'

'There are thin magnetic films of bubbles just below the surface of the shadows. When I burst a memory balloon, they pick up the vibrations in the air and orientate themselves to form pictures.'

'Like television?'

'More like a computer,' said Jidlaph. 'I slipped some of the memories into the memory of Rebekah that Isaac took from Gyrus. Isaac modified them somewhat, but they were reasonably accurate.'

'Think about her again, think about her.'

Laban turned away, 'I want to see her.' He picked up a stone from the path and hurled it at one of the balloons.

POP!

A scattering of raindrops fell down around them. They struck the path and flowed down into the river.

'Laban,' cried Jidlaph. 'What have you done?'

'Sorry,' said Laban, 'I need to see her.'

Jidlaph and Laban looked along the path as an image floated up in the shadow of a tree near them.

Fade In.

Scene 5: Int. French Café 'Le Puits', Year: 1995 – Night   5

ISAAC *sits at a small round table, a glass of Merlot in his hands. He nods at the girl sitting opposite, who talks of their plans for Christmas. A picture of Tournee du Chat Noir smiles down at them.*

GIRL   How about we go to my parents this Christmas and yours next year?

ISAAC   Sounds a good idea.

ISAAC *sips wine, looks around. His gaze stops at a young couple sitting in the corner. The man is talking. Every few minutes he stops with a gesture of hands, his arch movements throwing twisted shadows against the wall. ISAAC watches the waiter glance at the table. A single candle lights the face of the woman; she rubs her ear lobe, her eyes dart between the man before her and the door. Wisps of smoke from the candle snake up between the couple. ISAAC notices how the woman's fingers close around her drink, concealing the empty glass from the man's view.*

GIRL	Isaac, are you listening to me?
ISAAC	Yes of course.

ISAAC looks at the woman at the table again, her lips curl into a smile at the corners, she brings a strand of hair across her face as if to hide. The man laughs, she shuffles her feet, forces a smile, then notices ISAAC. She holds his gaze, candlelight flickering. The distance between them closes.

GIRL	So that's settled then?
ISAAC	Yes, fine.
GIRL	I need the bathroom.

The girl gets up and threads her way through tables. ISAAC finishes his wine and watches the waiter hand the couple in the corner the bill after a wild exclamation of 'l' addition,' from the man. The woman looks at ISAAC again; he feels lost, as the rest of the restaurant recedes into the background.

The man pushes his seat out, the scrapping sound breaks the hold over ISAAC and he realises time has passed, the bill is paid, the woman is leaving. The man leads the way out, the woman trails behind. ISAAC glances down as they pass his table. The woman pauses and sets her wineglass down before him. ISAAC follows the line of the glass to her smile. ISAAC'S pupils dilate; bliss flutters inward to take rest. Outside the world turns and she is gone. ISAAC holds the slender stem of the glass with his hand and turns the flute. A lipstick kiss curves around the bowl. His pulse racing he takes his napkin, wipes the lipstick from the glass, and pockets the kiss as his girlfriend returns to the table.

100

End of scene.

'Rebekah,' said Laban a tear forming in his eye, 'How do these memories help her?'

'By laying down an imprint in Isaac's mind that Rebekah can use as a place of safety to call Isaac upwards, if she manages to get out of Gyrus again.'

'Can't we just burst all the balloons now?'

'No,' said Jidlaph, 'they have to play in context for Isaac to remember them after playback. Now come, time is short.'

Laban followed Jidlaph down the path then stopped.

'*Think about her again, think about her.*'

Reaching down, Laban took a stone again and sent it towards a balloon above another tree.

'Laban!' shouted Jidlaph. 'You have to control yourself.'

POP!

Fade In.

Scene 6: Int. Bedroom – Christmas, Year: 1995 – Morning 6

ISAAC *wakes after his first night together with* REBEKAH. *He reaches over to place a hand around her. She is gone. He walks downstairs. There is no sign of her in the kitchen; he stuffs a mince pie, then walks to the lounge door. The smell of pine needles fills the air as he opens it, the open fire glows from the night before. On the floor is* REBEKAH. *She lies with pinecones around her, naked apart from a sheet of wrapping paper around her chest, another around her hips.*

ISAAC   Rebekah?

REBEKAH'S *eyes are closed; there is no response. He walks to her and looks at the snowmen smiling on the gift wrap. There is a tag attached to* REBEKAH'S *ring finger.* ISAAC *stoops down. It reads:*

Remember I am for life, not just for Xmas.
ISAAC *pulls* REBEKAH *up into his arms, the snowmen rustle.*

ISAAC   Wake up, Rebekah.

REBEKAH *opens her eyes; the Christmas Tree lights twinkle across her sleepy glaze.* ISAAC *kisses her.*

ISAAC   Good morning, Happy Christmas, I like my present.
REBEKAH   You do?
ISAAC   Subtle, is it a leap year?
REBEKAH   Well?
ISAAC   Yes, let's marry today, yesterday, all our days.

ISAAC *kisses her, laughing he rips the wrapping away.* REBEKAH *moves a pinecone from under her bottom.*

ISAAC (tracing his finger over Rebekah's breasts.) Your freckles trace out the constellation of the Little Bear.
REBEKAH   Do they?
ISAAC   I will marry you, Rebekah, and you will be my Little Bear.

REBEKAH *snarls, they entwine under the Christmas Tree; goose pimples on their skin, pinecones spinning on the floor.*

End of scene.

Laban looked up from the fading image on the path,
'We have to get her out.'
'Patience, Laban, you are destroying the memories every time you play one. Now follow me and don't touch anything.'
Jidlaph walked off down the path; Laban glanced up into the trees then followed. Eventually they reached the end of the

path. Jidlaph stopped and pointed up into the branches of the last tree.

'This one contains the memory of the car crash.'

'Why is there a fallen tree next to it?'

'That is the Dandelion Tree.'

'It's dead,' said Laban.

'It blew down in a storm the night of the crash. It will rise soon, Laban, we will sit here and wait.'

Isaac massaged his head. For a moment he caught glimpses of lipstick on a wineglass, pinecones spinning around Rebekah … then the memories faded and he stared ahead, the memories lost. It felt to Isaac as if he had been swimming naked in water that was dry against his skin. Reaching into his plastic bag, he took out the packet of paracetamol. With a loud gulp, he washed down four tablets with the coffee Deborah had left him. He sat trying to recall Rebekah again, but the pain dug into his brain.

Isaac turned and looked at Jacob propped up on the hospital bed. Jacob had been Rebekah's favourite of the twins, though she loved them both. She had bathed them every night and tucked them up with duvets and stories on cookie crumbed pillows. Esau had been Isaac's. Now Jacob was all that was left to show of their life together.

Isaac turned to the figurine of Buzz Lightyear on Jacob's bedside table. It was Jacob's favourite toy. The image calmed Isaac's thoughts and he pulled some lines of dialogue from his memory:

'Daddy, my Buzz isn't working.'

'Perhaps it needs new batteries, Jacob.'

'Like Mummy?'

'Mummy doesn't use batteries.'

'She does, I saw her putting one inside her.'

'That is the problem with memories,' thought Isaac, 'inappropriate intrusions, like Rebekah's vibrator. Not that it was wrong: but the timing, the timing.'

Isaac reached into his plastic bag, took out the packet of cookies and taking one placed it, like he did every day, on the pillow beside Jacob's head.

Isaac sighed then swallowed air. He struggled to speak as his Adam's apple bobbed back into position. He focused on the trees playing in the wind outside the window before he looked at Jacob again.

'Jacob, there's just you and me now. We've got to stick together okay?'

Jacob sat in his bed looking straight ahead. Nothing registered in his eyes. It had taken months for Isaac to get used to it. Jacob never focused on anything before him; the movement of Isaac pacing up and down the room talking to him forever unseen. Isaac had to choose to believe that somewhere deep within, lay his son. The doctors called it a 'persistent vegetative state.' It was a term Isaac hated. He felt it dehumanised his son with an insensitive label. The doctors also said Jacob had no chance of recovery.

And then Isaac noticed a tear forming in the corner of Jacob's eye. It swelled up and trickled down his cheek. Another followed and another, until Jacob sat crying silently. Isaac reached down, placed his hands behind his son's back and pulled him into an embrace. He sat there holding Jacob in his arms, rocking back and forth.

Finally tears for the loss of Rebekah fell, released by the tears of his distant son. Isaac laid Jacob back onto his pillow and looked at him. The light streaming in through the window flickered in the film of tears over Jacob's eyes and it seemed to Isaac that they were alive again. Reaching out his hand, Isaac dried Jacob's teardrops from his cheeks, 'Jacob?'

The light faded as clouds gathered.

Jacob stared out across his father's gaze.

Isaac cried for his son.

Chapter 12
On the Beach

The memory of Ishmael as a child rippled around the dark interior of his sticky fluid filled cell in HM Temporal Gyrus, muttering, 'Outcast,' his key phrase on his memory compression since the custodian, Phicol, had re-imprisoned him. He wanted to shout, 'Fable, I should be at the beach,' but, *outcast* was the only word he could speak.

With Ishmael compressed, the cell appeared empty, all that represented him both physically and emotionally, his whole being, was now represented by that one word inside Isaac's long term memory. For thirty-eight years that was all the childhood memory of Ishmael had ever known, then for a brief moment he was given life again by Fable.

'I can't do time again,' thought Ishmael, 'Please let me die, Isaac, forget me.'

A light forming in the darkness outside pulled Ishmael away from his thoughts. He pressed back into the corner of his cell and went quiet. The glow increased, until shafts of bright white light streamed through the bars.

The door to his cell swung open; Gabriel swam through and floated before him.

'Outcast,' said Ishmael, as if in explanation.

Gabriel looked at the disturbance in the fluid from the sound which gave away Ishmael's presence. Red, blue, and green points of light rose up within Gabriel's eyes; they rotated clockwise, stopped before they span anticlockwise unlocking the encryption. The red glow flared up sending a beam of red light out of Gabriel's eyes into the cell. The blue followed, then the green, until light bounced around like beams protecting some ancient treasure. The image of Ishmael formed where the light beams crossed.

'Hello, Ishmael,' said Gabriel.

Isaac gave form to Ishmael as his mind reconstructed the memory.

'Who are you?' said Ishmael.

'Do not be afraid,' said Gabriel. 'Quick, get up and follow me.'

Ishmael hesitated as Gabriel swam out of the cell, then kicking hard he followed through the maze of corridors.

At the entrance to the canteen hall, Ishmael pulled back. Two sentries sat sleeping, their muskets between their legs. Gabriel swam under the bubbles floating across the swing doors from their snoring. Ishmael took a gulp and followed through. He glanced back as the swing doors closed behind him and wondered if he had really passed the guards, or whether he was imagining it all and was still asleep inside his cell. As he swam past the site of the large willow tree, loose chains floated as iron seaweed that brushed against his feet.

'Where's the willow tree?'

'The custodians have brought it into play,' said Gabriel.

Ishmael shuddered and looked around. A small boy sat in a corner. Ishmael watched as the boy took a large chunk of bread and dipped it into a bowl of soup in front of him.

'Who's that?'

Gabriel turned to where Ishmael was pointing.

'Esau.'

'What's he doing out of his cell?'

'He's Isaac's favourite of the twins, the custodians let him eat here after he died in the crash – mostly he eats lentil soup.'

'Yuck.'

Gabriel sighed and carried on through the tunnel to the courtyard. Ishmael followed; they surfaced within the ring of pillars and doors. One of the doors opened and a Temporal prostitute swam out before the portcullis barring their way.

'Please help me.'

Ishmael looked at the Peter Brookes political cartoon covering her breasts, the small print of obituaries wrapped around her hips. Gabriel placed his hand on her shoulder and considered the half-completed crossword on her tummy.

'Shh,' said Gabriel, 'sleep now, Mahalath.'

Liquid gold flowed out from his fingers and ran over the girl's body. She gasped then went quiet.

'What have you done?' said Ishmael.

'She is asleep,' said Gabriel. 'Come.'

Ishmael swam around her, 'She looks familiar, have I met her?' He tapped her bottom with his fist.

CLUNK

'Stop it,' said Gabriel, 'you'll wake the sentries.'

'Sorry.'

Gabriel turned and faced the gate, 'Open.'

With a creak, the heavy, iron gate rose up, and they passed unchallenged into the parking lot.

Ishmael looked down at a line of new memories, two women at the front, caught his eye, one was dressed in a nurse's uniform, the other was naked and pregnant. They stood talking as the glow of Abimelech started to form. Ishmael stared entranced by the sight of nudity.

'That's Rebekah and Deborah,' said Gabriel.

'I know,' said Ishmael. 'How do I know that if I've never met them?'

'Who do you think is responsible for your consciousness?' said Gabriel.

'What?'

'Come on.'

They swam on over neurotransmitters. Hundreds became thousands, thousands millions.

'How many are there?' asked Ishmael.

'Over nine billion,' said Gabriel. 'There's more neurotransmitters here than the entire population of the planet.'

'Impressive, ' said Ishmael glancing back.

'Yes, as long as you don't forget where you parked,' said Gabriel.

Ishmael peered up at the sound of screeching from above. Heading towards them was the Relic Monger; the noise of its black bones scrapping against each other filled Ishmael's head.

'Quickly,' said Gabriel, 'it has smelt you, head towards the edge.'

Gabriel led Ishmael towards the outer rim of the parking lot. Darkness played over them cast from the wings of the Relic Monger like shifting shadows of branches on night windows.

Ishmael stopped at the edge and held his hand up against the outer membrane. Pushing his face up against it, he peered down. Far below the blue of the ocean followed the curvature of Isaac's mind.

'Now what?' said Ishmael, as the shrill squall of the Relic Monger screeched in his ears.

Gabriel took his hand, 'Jump.'

'What?'

Gabriel pushed through the wall, taking Ishmael with him.

'Ahh!'

Ishmael tumbled down through the sky with Gabriel. Above them the Relic Monger beat its wings against the outer limits of Temporal Gyrus and screamed.

Ishmael splashed down into the sea of Isaac's subconscious and bobbed to the surface. He looked around as Gabriel landed next to him; a line of sand stretched out without end behind him.

'The beach!' said Ishmael and started swimming to shore.

Below him shimmering fish mimicked his movements as he kicked his legs, until finally pulling away as Ishmael left deep water for the shallows.

Stepping from the waves onto the beach, Ishmael's feet disturbed footprints scattered across the swathes of sand obliterating intricate patterns marking out the history of the lost paradise.

'Watch yourself,' said Gabriel beside him.

Ishmael looked at him, then lifted his head as singing floating across the beach. Scanning around, he saw Isaac as a small boy playing by the waters edge.

'Bastard,' said Ishmael. 'Right.'

'No,' said Gabriel, 'I need to talk to him, you have something else you need to do don't you, Ishmael?'

Ishmael stared at him, 'What?'

'I think you know what you have decided to do, Ishmael, go now and do what you must.'

Ishmael remembered Fable's command to him, '*I want you to kill them when they reach the beach.*'

'I ...'

'Go,' said Gabriel and started to walk towards Isaac. Ishmael watched him for a moment then headed in the other direction.

'I'm at the beach, the beach!'

Ishmael walked with the sea lapping against his toes until he found sets of footprints leading out of the water.

'Mr Punch? Could be,' he thought, 'he's probably already here by now.'

Ishmael followed the footprints; they meandering up the beach and through an arch in an outcrop of rock. On the other side, Ishmael could just make out a group of people in the distance. An enormous red and white striped tent towered over them. Red, white and blue bunting flags attached to tie ropes, flapped in the sea breeze.

Ishmael flattened himself against the rock, took a deep breath, then walked over.

'Not now,' said the Devil as Ishmael approached. 'No show today, it's our day off.'

Ishmael looked at the cast of the Punch and Judy show, crouched around a Monopoly board.

'Hello,' said Mrs Punch.

'Er, hi,' said Ishmael, 'Can I play?'

He glanced around for Mr Punch and spotted him playing with a girl in the sea.

'Sure,' said Jack Ketch, the hangman, 'Come on, Scaramouche, get on with it.'

Scaramouche shook the dice in his hands and blew on them. They clinked and rattled together.

'Okay,' he said throwing the dice onto the board. 'Go, go go.'

'Finally the damn dice are on the board,' said the doctor.

The dice bobbled over the London streets, hit each other, spun around for a moment, and settled for a six and a five. Scaramouche moved his car forward to Old Kent Road.

'Brum, brum …right,' he said rubbing his hands, 'I'll buy it please.'

Mrs Punch sorted through the mass of cards, found Old Kent Road and passed it over.

'Thanks, I'll soon have hotels on these, so watch out everyone!'

'Well done, Scaramouche,' said Judy in her high pitched falsetto voice.

Scaramouche looked at Judy. The look lasted too long.

'Call me Hector, I don't think anyone remembers,' he whispered.

Judy smiled at him. Hector was the name of the horse that used to appear in the early days of the show. Only she knew it was Scaramouche under the horse's costume. She had once slipped under it with him during a performance.

'Wo, ho, Hector,' she whispered into Scaramouche's ear.

Scaramouche blushed and coughed.

'Your go, er, what did you say your name was?' said Mrs Punch as she watched her baby shove handfuls of sand into its mouth, 'Will you stop eating the beach!'

'I'm Ishmael.'

The baby stuck his tongue out at Mrs Punch. He had Scaramouche's nose and eyes.

'Funny name,' said Mrs Punch, 'sounds familiar, do we know you?'

'No, I don't think so.'

'Okay son, well throw the dice, there's a good boy.'

Clink clink clink … a four and a three.

Ishmael picked up a small card from the centre of the board. It had the word CHANCE written over it in bold letters.

He read it out, 'Go to jail. Move directly to jail. Do not pass go. Do not collect £200.00.'

'Never mind son,' said the blind man.

Further down the beach, Gabriel sat talking to the memory of Isaac as a five-year-old child.

'... and next time,' said Gabriel, 'check with me before helping a high security memory escape like that.'

'Sorry,' said Isaac, 'Fable said I would be helping.'

'It's okay, I think you may have actually done some good.'

Isaac looked past Gabriel and fell to his knees.

'Quick,' he said scooping sand into his spade.

'Got it,' said Gabriel. He dug his hands into the beach and shovelled sand onto the wall in front of him.

'Do you think we can beat it?' said Isaac.

'Beat the sea? Probably not.'

Isaac let the spade fall from his hands.

'But,' said Gabriel peering out from his grey hood, 'that doesn't stop us from trying.'

Isaac smiled and picking up his spade, he tipped some sand onto the top of the wall. A wave reared up against it. The wall held.

Gabriel worked quickly and before long Isaac was surrounded by a ring of sandy battlements awaiting the onslaught. Isaac had contributed a few more spades full himself and sat smiling, a small Action Man beside him dressed as a British Navy sailor.

The sea continued up the beach and swirled around the protective walls of the castle. As the watery assault grew fiercer, Gabriel and Isaac repaired any breach in their defences. The tide carried up the beach behind them. The castle held.

Gabriel turned and looked at Isaac, 'I have to go soon. A few more minutes and then it's time to say goodbye.'

'Are you God?' said Isaac.

'My name is Gabriel.'

'Will you come and play with me again?'

Gabriel fell silent and stared out to sea. Turning to Isaac he said, 'No. I'm sorry.'

'Please,' said Isaac.

Gabriel took both Isaac's hands and peered into his eyes.

'Isaac, I want you to know I have always been your friend.'

'Can I stay a few more minutes,' said Isaac.

'One more minute,' said Gabriel.

Isaac watched as a large wave broke over the main wall. It picked up his small Action Man and rammed it against the back wall. Isaac gasped. Getting up, he ran to save his toy. Gabriel watched as he picked it up. Isaac hugged it and held it close to his chest.

Isaac sat down next to Gabriel. Gabriel put his arms around him as Isaac snuggled up to him.

'Do I have to go back there?' said Isaac. 'It's so dark and the custodians scare me. Why don't my mummy and daddy come for me?'

A tear formed in the corner of Gabriel's eye. It dripped down and disappeared into the sand.

'Listen little man, be strong. You have to go back now, your empty cell will be discovered.'

The waves grew stronger and clawed over the walls around them. A pool of water started to fill up around their legs. The wet sand from the top of the battlements slumped down as the sea cut away the footings from under it. Within moments, the wall breached. Isaac took a step back. Gabriel looked at the mounting waves.

'Minutes up. Isaac, I forgive you for what you are about to do. It has been my privilege to protect you.'

Isaac looked at him and squeezed his hand.

A large wave rolled up and caught hold of him. Gabriel held onto him for a moment then uncurling his fingers he let go. The wave swept Isaac out into the deep blue water. His Action Man held tight in his clasp.

Chapter 13
The Region of Moriah

Isaac reached over and pivoted the television monitor around so he could see the screen. An advert for death insurance was playing.

'For Christ sakes,' said Isaac, and started flicking through the channels. He stopped at a Danger Mouse cartoon, pushed the screen back and placed the headphones around Jacob's head. He looked up at the sound of a knock at the door. The handle turned, the door opened with a squeak and Gabriel stepped through.

'Hello, Isaac.'

'Do I know you?'

'Yes, I sang over you when you were young,' said Gabriel.

'I'm sorry? Are you a friend of my father?'

'Yes, Abe and I are good friends,' said Gabriel. 'So how do you feel about remembering Rebekah?'

'Excuse me?' said Isaac.

'She wasn't a Goddess, Isaac. That you should elevate her such is understandable though.'

'What did you just say?' said Isaac staring at Gabriel.

'Isaac, my time is short. I want to say goodbye and I want to give you something.'

'Are you another memory,' said Isaac. 'Am I going mad?'

'No, I am Gabriel and possibly, it depends.'

'So if I signalled the nurse to come, she would see you as well?'

'That would be Deborah? She pointed out your room for me, she smiled at the mention of your name.'

Isaac looked at his feet, 'What do you want to give me?'

'A memory of you that came from Rebekah.'

'How can you do that?'

Gabriel strode forward and placed his hand on the front of Isaac's head. Isaac's world stopped. In his mind an image started to form …

Fade In:

Scene 1: Ext. Mamre Wood, Year: 1997 – Day   1

REBEKAH *and* ISAAC *sit under the shade of the Dandelion Tree. Around them are a wicker picnic hamper, two half emptied flutes, a champagne bottle sitting in a cooler box. They are both dressed casually.* ISAAC *wears a pair of stonewashed jeans; they hang straight, yet ruffle as they reach his black boots. A white shirt, half tucked in, covers his chest. The bottom button is left undone, showing a triangular shaped patch of brown stomach. A well tailored jacket sits square on his shoulders, the heavy cloth giving a razor edge to its line.* REBEKAH *wears a pair of frayed blue denim shorts, which sit low on her hips; an ocean horizon with a naked sky above and a Jacques Cousteau mysterious world below. The top of her blouse is held together by a cotton lattice. A gold nose stud punches through her left nostril. Her lips, red, are closed; her head tipped back. She raises her hand, sweeps back hair from her face and twists the strands around each other with fingers that fiddle with split ends.*

REBEKAH   I love it here.

ISAAC   This is where I used to come as a small boy, when I wanted to be alone.

REBEKAH *smiles, and takes a bag of* FATBISCUIT *cookies from the hamper. She chooses one encrusted with large dark chunks of chocolate the size of golf balls and washes it down with her flute of bubbles.*

ISAAC   When I grew older, I used to imagine being here with my girlfriend. We'd kiss and share secrets together. It never happened of course.

REBEKAH   Until now.

ISAAC   Until now. (He kisses Rebekah) Tell me a secret then.

REBEKAH   When I was seventeen ... (she glances at Isaac) ... we were poor, you must remember that.

ISAAC   Go on.

REBEKAH   Well I was out shopping with my girlfriend and we decided to buy our first Wonderbra. We wanted the *Hello, Boys* look.

ISAAC   Eva Herzigova.

REBEKAH   Yes.

ISAAC   Is it wrong that I am starting to feel aroused?

REBEKAH   (laughs) The problem was we had no money.

ISAAC   You stole them?

REBEKAH   Er … yes, you are the first person I've ever told, I felt guilty for months.

ISAAC   Did it work?

REBEKAH   What?

ISAAC   The Wonderbra. Did you look like the poster?

REBEKAH   Yes, are you listening to me? You seem to be still stuck on Eva.

ISAAC   Sorry.

REBEKAH *sighs, wipes the chocolate from her lips and looks into* ISAAC'S *eyes.*

REBEKAH   Come on then you tell me a secret.

ISAAC   Okay. When I was six, I climbed this tree for the first time. When I got to the top, I saw people flying above me.

REBEKAH   And you since discovered the marvel of aeroplanes?

ISAAC   No, Rebekah, they were flying. It was like I was dreaming and flying with them. They gave me chocolate and sang to me.

REBEKAH   Hmm … did they have wings?

ISAAC   No.

REBEKAH   No wings? Pity …

ISAAC   What's wrong?

REBEKAH   I wish I could still believe in my childhood fantasies.

ISAAC   Come on, let's climb up right now and I'll show you.

REBEKAH   No, Isaac. Stop trying to fix me all the time.

ISAAC   No, come on. Let me show you.

REBEKAH   (sighs) Okay.

ISAAC   You have to believe though. You won't see anything. Not if you don't believe.

REBEKAH   Okay, let's get it over with.

REBEKAH *and* ISAAC *climb the crocodile ladder. They see nothing. They climb down.* REBEKAH *looks at* ISAAC.

REBEKAH   I guess that's two of us that don't believe anymore then.

A north wind starts to blow against the side of REBEKAH'S *face. It is joined by a cool wind from the south. Rain starts falling. The first drops hit the side of their champagne flutes, which reply by ringing out with accompanying pings. The drops roll down the mouths of the crystal and disappear into the liquid. The rain grows heavy. It smashes into their picnic and flows over them. The sweet fragrance of wet grass floats up around them.* REBEKAH *and* ISAAC *stand in the rain and fight the instinct to flee.* REBEKAH *reaches out and runs her finger down the scar under* ISAAC'S *eye. As she does, a blinding white light fills her vision. It fades and she looks around. She is standing on a large open space of ground. A large mountain rears up out of the shimmering haze in the distance.* ISAAC *is nowhere to be seen.*

REBEKAH   What the?

GABRIEL   Hello, Rebekah.

REBEKAH *spins around and looks at* GABRIEL.

REBEKAH   Where am I? I know you don't I? ... Is it Gabriel?

GABRIEL   Yes I was at your wedding; we spoke about the weather if I recall.

REBEKAH   What's happened to me? Am I dead? Are you ... are you an angel?

GABRIEL   You have a bit of chocolate under your lip.

REBEKAH   What? O ... thank you.

GABRIEL   Let us sit together, Rebekah.

REBEKAH *twitches her fingers against her thigh as if going for the grip of a Smith & Wesson. She sits on the floor. It is dry and dusty.*

GABRIEL   You touched Isaac's scar under the Dandelion Tree.

REBEKAH   So?

GABRIEL   Everyone has hidden in their physical make up a story that shapes who they are. Few are aware of the existence of such marks. Fewer still get to read them.

REBEKAH   What?

GABRIEL   Your love for Isaac is intense under these branches. You see clearly his tenderness and strength that you find so attractive. It has enabled you to unlock a story from his past by your touch. Such stories are deeply personal and rarely shared between two people.

REBEKAH   Am I inside the story?

GABRIEL   Yes. Watch ...

The image of the plains flicker around REBEKAH. GABRIEL *starts to narrate the story. His words condense into pictures.* REBEKAH *watches as the images of* ISAAC *and* ISHMAEL *form before her. The ground under her feet starts to shake as two vast armies march towards them across the plains. Those from the north line up behind* ISAAC. *Those from the south form ranks behind*

117

ISHMAEL, *who is older, taller. The brothers stare at each other unaware of the men of fire around them. Those behind* ISHMAEL *drop down on one knee and pull back on their long bows. Those behind* ISAAC *are dressed in armour with an emblem of a tree on their breastplates. The sound of swords banging against shields fills the air.*

ISAAC   Give me back my Action Man!
ISHMAEL   No.
ISAAC   Why are you always picking on me? Give him back or I'll tell Mum.
ISHMAEL   O so scared. You and your mum make me sick. You think you are so much better than us, but one day Dad will leave her and take us away with him.

REBEKAH *looks down at* ISHMAEL'S *hand as* GABRIEL *describes the small knife clutched in it. It is* ABE'S *knife.* ISHMAEL *raises his arm and points the knife towards* ISAAC. *The army of archers point their black arrows skyward.*

ISHMAEL   Swear allegiance to me, little half-brother and I'll put this away.
ISAAC   I'm not scared of you. You wouldn't dare!
ISHMAEL   Wanna bet.

REBEKAH *looks up as she hears distant singing. The sound fills the expanse of blue above. Each word is accompanied by a musical echo of its form which fills the air with music.* REBEKAH *hears the alternating sounds of harps and lyres. She feels a blast of wind against her face as she hears each.* GABRIEL *describes how it starts to rain in the story. His words float up into the sky and stream apart into millions of raindrops. They fall over the scene. As each drop hits* REBEKAH, *it forms the word raindrop. She remains dry as the words flow down over her and disappear into the dirt around her feet.*

118

ISAAC   Give him back.

ISHMAEL *turns the blade towards the Action Man. The rain dashes against it as if to throw it from his grasp. He brings it across towards the Action Man's throat. The blade slices through the thudding rain.* ISHMAEL *starts to press the cold blade into the plastic.* ISAAC *shouts and runs at* ISHMAEL. *The two brothers collide, water splashes up into the air, the Action Man falls to the ground.* ISAAC *grasps* ISHMAEL'S *hand and struggles against the blade.* REBEKAH *screams and runs to them. She tries to grasp hold of* ISHMAEL'S *hand. The image flickers at the point of contact as her hand passes through. Tiny black words describing the anatomy of* ISHMAEL'S *hand, float down from the disturbance.*

ISAAC   (crying) Let go of the knife.

ISHMAEL *swipes at* ISAAC, REBEKAH *looks up as the tip of the blade passes through her and enters the side of* ISAAC'S *face. There is the sound of steel against bone. A thin line of red follows the blade, which stops just short of plunging into the white of* ISAAC'S *eye. Thousands of arrows flame over their heads to accompany the strike. A shadow falls over them all as the swarm blocks out the sun.* REBEKAH *turns and watches them rain down onto the army behind* ISAAC. *Whole lines of soldiers fall.*

ISAAC   You cut me!

ISHMAEL *pushes;* ISAAC *dodges, stumbles, falls.* ISHMAEL *places a foot on his stomach and squats down.*

ISHMAEL   Now little brother, it's time for your rite of passage.

ISHMAEL *pulls* ISAAC'S *trousers down.* ISAAC *screams and thrashes as* ISHMAEL *rips his boxers away.*

ISHMAEL   Hold still you little runt. Now you know what you father spared you from, what I had to endure? No?

ISHMAEL *takes the blade and holds it before* ISAAC'S *face.*

ISHMAEL   Circumcision, Isaac. Do you think this is sharp enough to remove your foreskin?
ISAAC   Please, Ishmael, don't.
ISHMAEL   And God said, every male among you shall be circumcised.

ISHMAEL *lowers the blade and prepares to cut.* ISAAC *goes still and starts crying.* REBEKAH *looks away. Suddenly the thick hand of* ABE *clasps around* ISHMAEL'S *hand.*

ISHMAEL   Father! Isaac stole your knife; I have it for you.
ABE   Walk to the house; wait for me there.
ISHAMEL   But, Father.
ABE   (shouting.) To the house.

ISHMAEL *drops the knife and runs towards Mamre House. The army of swordsman parts to allow him through.* ISAAC *watches as his brother disappears from view across the plains of Moriah.* ABE *pulls* ISAAC'S *trousers back up, picks him up and cradles him in his arms. A tear forms in* ISAAC'S *eye.* REBEKAH *looks into* GABRIEL'S *eyes as he stops talking. The image there of* ABE *and* ISAAC *flickers and fades. The two armies turn and withdraw. Tears roll down* REBEKAH'S *face.* GABRIEL *leans forward and wipes them away.*

REBEKAH   They really hate each other don't they?
GABRIEL   Yes.
REBEKAH   Does it hurt him?

GABRIEL   Yes, Ishmael is his only brother. Within him is the need for things to be made right between the two of them.

REBEKAH   What were the armies all about? Did that part really happen?

GABRIEL   You are not ready for the answer to those questions. I have been allowed only to show you them.

REBEKAH *starts to speak, then stops. She sighs and asks.*

REBEKAH   How can he forgive that?

GABRIEL   He cannot bury the hurt; he needs to forgive so that he can cast it aside.

REBEKAH   Why hasn't he spoken of it?

GABRIEL   He is a proud man.

REBEKAH   Can I help him?

GABRIEL   No, he needs to forgive Ishmael. It is a choice only he can make. They shall fight again with death and sickness surrounding them on all sides before that time.

REBEKAH   How-

GABRIEL *places his finger over* REBEKAH'S *mouth to silence her questions.*

GABRIEL   Shh. Rebekah, let's talk about you.

REBEKAH   Me?

GABRIEL   You wish to become pregnant, but you can't.

REBEKAH   I ... I ...yes.

GABRIEL   You shall give birth to twins, Rebekah. Do you think you can believe that?

REBEKAH   I don't know.

REBEKAH *looks into* GABRIEL'S *eyes and sees her reflection in them. She appears different in the image. She looks happy, radiant, alive.*

121

REBEKAH   Gabriel, why does it feel so good under here in Mamre Wood?

GABRIEL   I think garden is a better way of describing it, Rebekah.

A white light flares up again in front of REBEKAH. It fades and she is back before ISAAC in Mamre Wood. She looks at him for a moment, her eyes shimmering. They pull into each other and kiss.

ISAAC   Rebekah, I love you.   Let's get wet together.

REBEKAH *sees the glint in his eyes and starts to unlace the chord to her top. She pulls it off over her head. The cotton falls onto the grass around her feet. She unclips her bra and feels the touch of cold air ripple over her nipples. Reaching down she places her thumb beneath the elastic of her knickers and puckers down the material to reveal the effect of a painful wax.* ISAAC *pulls his jacket off, undoes his shirt buttons and takes his wet shirt off.* REBEKAH *looks at him and laughs. He has shaved his chest. Raindrops strike down onto his smooth skin.* ISAAC *undoes the silver buckle to his trousers and undresses.* REBEKAH *looks at* ISAAC'S *foreskin pulled back by his erection, then at the Dandelion Tree behind him. The long grass and the circle of old sycamores dance in the wind around them.*

REBEKAH   Garden? The Garden?
ISAAC   What did you say?

REBEKAH *places her hand into* ISAAC'S.

REBEKAH   Let's explore this garden.
ISAAC   Now? Naked?
REBEKAH   Yes. Come on.

REBEKAH *runs off laughing. She leaps like the fawn of a gazelle through the high grass, her breasts bouncing with the rhythm. She looks behind her and sees* ISAAC *hesitate for a second before giving chase, his erection bobbing, a heat seeking missile with its guidance system failing. He catches her under a pear tree.*

REBEKAH   (breathless) Okay okay.

REBEKAH *laughs as they settle down into the grass together.* ISAAC *nuzzles into* REBEKAH'S *breasts; her nipples like fruit pastels in his mouth.* REBEKAH *sighs; the wood swirls into Paisley print: around them daisies lift into the air. They join together in a circular embrace to form a ring of summer droplets which float up into the sky.*

End of scene.

'Rebekah,' said Isaac, 'so that's why you started to believe-'
Isaac looked at Gabriel.
'She saw you at the tree?'
'Yes.'
'I had stopped believing in you.'
'I know, but I continued to exist anyway.'
Isaac placed his head into his hands.
'Ishmael was sent away by father, if he can't forgive then why should I?'
The sound of swords beating against shields echoed around his head in time with the beat of his headache.
Bang, bang, bang.
'You believe that Abe sent him away because of what happened to you?' said Gabriel.
'Of course.'
Isaac felt his head explode outward. Pieces of memories, dreams, hopes, blasting through flesh.
'What is happening to me?' he said through gritted teeth.

'You died in your mind as Donaldson. Your body is following suit.'

'Rubbish, this isn't real; I have created you out of my madness.'

Gabriel took a step forward and reached out his hand to place it on Isaac's shoulder.

'Get away from me,' said Isaac. He fell back into his chair and looked down at the floor. The pain intensified; he felt faint. The floor started to spin. Isaac forced his last words out as if globs of toothpaste squeezed from the dregs of a rolled up tube, 'Go - to -'

Isaac's eyelids came down as guillotines. The last word fell from his lips and sank down into the floor ...

-Hell-

Isaac's head fell forward. He staggered, hit the ground.

Gabriel looked at Isaac sprawled out motionless. Stepping around him, he placed his hands on Jacob's forehead.

A picture of the Dandelion Tree flashed for a second across Jacob's eyes. Jacob made a sighing noise through his dry lips. His eyelids fluttered and the image descended.

Chapter 14
Remember

Ishmael watched Mr Punch and Pretty Polly frolic in the water as he languished in jail on the Monopoly board. In his pocket he felt the sharp blade of his knife against his finger. Next to him sat Scaramouche, who was looking at the policeman.

'I'm out of money,' said the blind man to the policeman. 'I can't pay you.'

'You cheat,' said Scaramouche grabbing the policeman's black book. Monopoly cards fell from the open pages as he threw it to the floor.

'Steady, Scaramouche,' said the policeman, 'remember who you are dealing with.'

Scaramouche laughed, got to his feet and kicked the Monopoly board high into the air. Plastic houses and metal icons spun; cards took flight as if a flock of startled birds.

'You stupid idiot,' said the Devil, 'you've ruined the game.'

Scaramouche shrugged and looked up as a tiny yellow card fluttered down past his nose. Reaching out his hand he caught it:

CHANCE: You are assessed for Street Repairs. £40.00 Per House. £115 Per Hotel.

The policeman laughed, Scaramouche ignored him and turned to Judy.

'Let me entertain you, Judy.'

Standing up, Scaramouche reached into his pocket and pulled out a pair of walnut wood castanets. Taking a step closer to Judy he started striking his heels down on the sand.

CLICK, CLICK, CLICK went the castanets at the courtship dance.

Ishmael reached over and picked up the policeman's notebook. He flipped through the white pages looking at the line drawings of Pretty Polly as Scaramouche danced.

'Heh,' shouted the policeman, 'that's mine, boy.'

'They're all mad,' thought Ishmael. 'I can't have them on my beach, I'm going to have to kill them.'

He handed the book to the policeman and got to his feet.

'I'll start with Punch,' he thought and walked down towards the sea.

He stopped at the waters edge and peered out. Thousands of lights skimmed across the surface of the water like fairy lights strung out as a net over the sea. Ishmael pulled out his knife and looked up at the bubbles floating into the sky on the horizon. He dropped his face, looked at his feet. The wet sand around them reflected the light of the day. Particles of sand bobbled past his toes as a wave slid back down into the sea making a 'shh' sound. An incoming wave answered by pushing it back up the beach with a 'whoosh'.

Ishmael looked as the water dragged the sand away to reveal the tip of a bottle. He stepped forward into the waves and stooping down picked the bottle up. It was white with a blue sailing boat on it; a small star on its stopper. He pulled the stopper out and stepped back as the voice of Abe flowed out of it.

'What on earth were you thinking?'

Ishmael tipped the bottle upside down and tapped it with his knife.

'Father?'

Ishmael shook his head. Before him the sea became an auditorium of water surging back with the tide to watch the climax to the second act. Punch and Pretty Polly were swimming back to their seats after the low tide interval. Ishmael dropped the bottle and began striding through the waves towards them.

He froze as he felt something brush up against his feet.

'What the?'

He jumped back. A body lay face down in the water. Ishmael pocketed his knife, grabbed the body and dragged it through the waves to shore. Before him the fairy lights across the water became spotlights shining up onto the stage.

The rest of the gang ran down to look. Ishmael rolled the body over. Sand covered a black gas mask, upper body armour was strapped over a black jump suit.

'Is he dead?' said Mrs Punch.

'Looks like it,' said Ishmael turning around. 'Look, he's got a hole in his forehead.'

'He looks kind of scary,' said Judy.

Ishmael reached down and pulled off the mask. The face of Isaac stared upwards. A scar ran down below his right eye. Ishmael stared at it, his knife heavy in his pocket.

'Stand back please.'

The gang looked behind them to see who had spoken.

'Gabriel!' said Ishmael.

'Hello, Ishmael.'

'What happened, did you kill Isaac?'

Gabriel shook his head and took a step towards the fallen body. The blind man shuffled up and stood leaning on his staff blocking his path.

'Excuse me,' said Gabriel.

'Can you spare some money?' said the blind man. He coughed and showered Gabriel in a stream of spit.

Gabriel wiped the saliva from his face with the back of his sleeve.

'Get out of the way, you old fool,' said the doctor.

'No. It's okay,' said Gabriel. He swirled his mouth around with a glooping sound, then spat in the face of the blind man.

'Flippin' heck,' said Jack Ketch, 'a gob fight. Stand back everyone, watch out for stray bullets.'

The blind man wiped the spit from his eyelids, spat back at Gabriel and raised his long staff to strike. Shades of blue stayed his arm. Touches of yellow released his grip on his staff. Shapes found definition and the blind man stood staring wide-eyed at his surroundings.

'I ... I ... it's beautiful,' he said. 'Thank you. Who are you that you restore an old man's sight?'

Gabriel smiled at the blind man.

'I knew it,' said the doctor. 'You old faker!'

Gabriel bent down and placed his hands on Isaac's upper chest. The gang watched as the waves lapped over his fingers. Clusters of bubbles started forming. With each wave, came more, until the whole of Isaac's body was covered in tiny bubbles glinting in the light.

'Is he shampooing him?' said Scaramouche.

'Shh,' said Mrs Punch.

Standing up, Gabriel filled his lungs and blew over Isaac. The bubbles lifted into the air. Ishmael looked back down at his brother lying in the wet sand. The hole in Isaac's head had gone; stirring, Isaac rubbed his forehead, then pushed himself up.

In the hospital, Isaac stirred. His brittle heart finding its normal rhythm again. He got to his feet. Gabriel stood looking out of the window. Half dazed and with images of Rebekah in the hotel apartment the day of Jacob's conception, Isaac picked up the phone.

'Humour me one last time,' said the voice of Rebekah in the room.

'Hello, Patient Line.'

'Yes,' said Isaac, 'can I have a chilled bottle of champagne and two glasses sent to room nineteen.'

'Sorry?'

Inside his head, on the beach, Isaac found his voice again.

'Where ...where am I?'

He tried to bring the scene into focus. Gabriel reached down and pulled him to his feet.

'Hello, Isaac.'

'Donaldson, my name's Donaldson,' said Isaac.

'Really?' said Gabriel.

Isaac looked at Gabriel, then reaching into his holster he pulled out his pistol and pushed it into the side of Gabriel's face. Ishmael drew back.

'Where's the rest of my team? Where am I?'

128

'We will start,' said Gabriel, 'with who you are.'

Donaldson frowned. 'I know who I am, who are you?'

'As you please. My friends call me Gabriel. Now what is far more important is who are you?'

Isaac tensed his trigger figure. Drips of sweat formed on his brow and trickled down his face. His heart rate increased. Music floated across the beach. It was 'Ocean Rain' by Echo and the Bunnymen.

'I ... I am Donaldson. Tom Donaldson.' he mouthed through his lips.

'Isaac, don't you remember me? It's Ishmael, your brother,' said Ishmael.

Isaac glanced at Ishmael, then at Gabriel again.

'You had a beautiful wife called Rebekah and two little boys, Jacob and Esau,' said Gabriel. 'Rebekah and Esau died last year, Jacob lies asleep.'

'Rebekah?' said Isaac as he remembered falling onto the tarmac at the airport, 'No, I lost focus, I have no wife and kids.'

'Reach deep inside and ask yourself if that's true,' said Gabriel.

'No, I don't want to,' said Isaac. Waves broke behind him, sending the sound of Blur's 'This is a Low' over him.

'Isaac,' said Gabriel.

Isaac slumped onto the sand, as the music took him back to the car crash.

'Isaac,' repeated Gabriel.

'Yes.'

'Let Donaldson go, you can't heal the pain of the crash with the creation of this delusion.'

'No,' he said forcing down tears. He got to his feet and levelled his pistol at Gabriel's head.

'Where the fuck am I?'

'Isaac, you're making it worse.'

'Shut up and answer me.'

'You are within the beach, in your mind.'

'Why does this child call me brother?'

'Because I am, Isaac,' said Ishmael, 'Abe is our father.'

Isaac turned his gun towards Ishmael.

'Stop, he's just a kid,' said Mrs Punch.

Ishmael took his knife from his pocket and held it against Isaac's scar, 'Remember this, Isaac?'

'Let go of the knife,' said Isaac.

'Put the gun down,' said Ishmael.

'Don't you mean, *hold still you little runt?*' said Isaac and squeezed the trigger.

'No Isaac!' screamed Mrs Punch.

The bullet exited the gun and punched through Ishmael's throat. He dropped the knife and fell.

'Please, Isaac,' said Ishmael, struggling to look up.

Isaac looked at his brother and sent another shot through his head.

Ishmael slumped dead onto the sand.

'Why didn't you stop him?' said Mrs Punch at Gabriel.

'Excuse me, sir,' said Scaramouche, 'you are upsetting the lady.'

Isaac turned, lifted his smoking gun and shot Scaramouche through the chest.

Mrs Punch screamed and dropped to her lover.

Gabriel looked at Isaac, 'When does it stop, Isaac?'

Outside the hospital a flock of birds soared on the thermals. They banked in unison, sunlight flashing from their white feathers as if a school of fish across open waters. Gabriel watched their shifting patterns in the sky, turning he looked at Isaac. The reflection of the monitor's red lights flashed in his eyes.

At Bethuel's Leap, the fallen Dandelion Tree rose up before Laban and Jidlaph.

'It's time,' said Jidlaph and climbed the tree.

Moments later he reappeared from its branches.

'We must go back,' said Jidlaph.

'What?'

'There's a memory implanted at the start of things, hidden amongst the memories of Rebekah.'

In the courtyard of Temporal Gyrus, Abimelech swam around the golden statue of the prostitute. The sentries stood in front of their doors looking at the golden crossword emblazed on her stomach, pencils gripped in their old fingers. Abimelech wrapped a tentacle around one of the statue's arms and turned to face them.

'What is it that threatens a man that he should mutilate the body of a woman?'

Abimelech squeezed his tentacle and snapped off her arm, 'Is it that he fears she will beat him in an arm wrestle?' Her golden arm sank to the floor, Abimelech broke off her other arm, 'There now, isn't that better, Mahalath, daughter of Ishmael?'

At Isaac's house in another time and place, the adult version of Ishmael strode to his car. He opened the door and looked at the drops of water that lay across the dancing horse logo on the bonnet. He turned the key in the ignition and the twin exhausts pumped out smoke into the air. Echo and the Bunnymen's 'Bring On The Dancing Horses' floated up out of the car. The wheels kicked up the gravel as he drove past the golden trees and through the gate onto the plains of Morah.

'Why don't you stop it all?' said Isaac.

'That is for you to do,' said Gabriel. He lowered his arm and placed it on the doctor, who crouched over the dead body of Scaramouche.

'Remember.'

Isaac flinched at the words, and pointed the gun at Gabriel's head.

'I,' said Isaac looking at Gabriel, 'don't believe anymore.'

Isaac's right finger pulled at the trigger. Gabriel watched the hammer spur fall, heard the sound of bullet leaving muzzle, heard the policeman quoting Isaac his Miranda rights, 'You have the right to remain silent. If you give up the right to-'

A puff of smoke exited the barrel of the gun and swirled behind the racing bullet.

Gabriel rose up from the sand. Behind him the canvas of the red and white striped tent billowed in the wind and tore at the pegs in the sand.

Memories flashed across Gabriel's mind.

Isaac being swept out to sea.

The look on the Temporal prostitute's face.

Ishmael and Rebekah under the Dandelion Tree.

Isaac's house in flames.

Isaac embracing his children, kissing Rebekah.

The cry of a newborn child in Isaac's arms.

The commission to Mary in Aramaic. *Do not be afraid, Mary, you have found favour with God. You will be with child and give birth to a son, and you are to give him the name-*

Thwack. The bullet pierced Gabriel's heart.

Gabriel coughed blood and clutched at his chest. He struggled to finish the sentence in his mind:

'Jesus,' he gasped, the words tender on his dying lips.

Gabriel coughed and spluttered and looked for the last time at Isaac.

The waves stopped. The beach went from yellow to steel grey as the light faded.

In the hospital, Gabriel's eyes shot forward three beams of light. They danced around the hospital room and flickered over the monitoring equipment showing the rise and fall of Jacob's heartbeat in a stream of green code. As Jacob's heart monitor peaked, the machine gave out a reassuring noise. The light fell away as it followed the rhythm; Gabriel's eyes dimmed and went dark. He slumped to the floor. The noise from the heart monitor slowed, stopped.

Isaac opened his mouth; no words came from his moving lips. He turned his head alarmed at the silence. The trace still showed a regular beat; yet no sound came from the machine. Isaac looked at the television. No sound accompanied the moving pictures. Isaac started towards Gabriel then stopped as the flow of time in the room paused to take in the event. Outside the traffic flowed quietly by for a moment, then became still.

The sun sat motionless above them hanging in drapes of blue and white.

On the beach, the baby started to cry. Judy nestled him in her arms. Tears rolled down her face as she looked at the dead body of Scaramouche. She kissed her baby.

'Shh,' my darling, 'it's going to be okay, look.'

Behind Isaac a figure strode out of the waves. The baby gurgled in delight as his father looked up the beach at him.

'Shall I?' he mouthed to his child.

The baby nodded.

Isaac span around and saw Punch standing behind him.

'Huzza! Huzza!' Punch cried and whacked his stick down on top of his head.

Isaac lost consciousness and fell headfirst into the wet sand.

'That's the way to do it! That's the way to do it!' shouted Punch as he jumped up and down.

Pretty Polly walked out of the sea behind him dressed in her peach bra and knickers. She wrapped her arms around Punch.

'My hero,' she said and kissed him on the side of his face.

Judy glared at her through her tears.

Punch sang as he grabbed hold of Pretty Polly's hands and swirled her around in a dance.

A huge wave rolled up the beach towards them. It broke and crashed down around the body of Gabriel. With a loud sucking noise, it dragged Gabriel down into the sea in its backwash.

Far up in the atmosphere, all Isaac's thoughts ruptured. Water thrashed down onto the surface of the sea and pitted into the smooth surface. Gabriel floated in the drumming of the rain as the swell of the water pitched him up and down. Lightning flashed as

133

he finally sank into the cold darkness below. As he neared the bottom, the bubbles that had come together to give him a physical body inside Isaac's mind, pulled away. The definition in Gabriel's outline faded. The school of silver bubbles streamed outwards, mourning the form they once held.

Act 3
The Dandelion Tree

Chapter 15
Revelation

Plaster and brick soaked in human anguish formed the four walls
to Jacob's room. Hairline cracks snaked from the lemon ceiling.
Silence continued; then the sound of Jacob's monitor started
again; waves of sound rippled up from the floor from Isaac's
footsteps.

'Where's Gabriel?'

Isaac looked around, Gabriel had disappeared.

A small chunk of plaster fell from the wall. It shattered as
it hit the floor and sent a puff of dust up into the room. Soft red
brick showed through the damage. Isaac stared at it as he rubbed
his aching stomach, his mind whirled; the pain increased and his
thoughts slipped under the madness of Mr Punch's singing:

> *Killed by his own folly.*
> *And of Rebekah, Esau and Isaac?*
> *Never to reach them, falling, falling.*

Isaac tried to reach out to something to steady his mind.

'My car,' he thought, 'I'm in my car, I'm feeling safe and
secure within. I am in control.'

'Proceed straight ahead,' said his sat-nav in a female voice.

Isaac walked towards the hole in the plaster.

'Turn left at the next junction.'

Isaac turned as he reached the wall.

'Take the next right.'

Isaac walked through the door to the bathroom.

'You have arrived at your destination.'

Isaac blinked; through his imaginary windscreen he could
see the toilet.

'I need the toilet,' he thought and pulled back his hospital
gown.

'Ahh, that's better,' he said, at the sound of tinkling in the
enamel.

'Error,' said the sat-nav. 'Please turn around at the next
opportunity.'

Isaac span around and showered the bathroom in urine. He finished, tucked himself back into his boxer shorts and stared into the mirror above the sink.

'You have arrived at your destination,' said the sat-nav.

'Good,' said Isaac.

As he stood in the pool of processed coffee, Isaac examined the scar under his eye. Reaching down, he rummaged through his overnight bag he kept there for emergencies. Finding his razor, he flipped back the restrainer and removed the blade. He ran his finger down the sharp edge, then held it at the top of his scar. His hand started to shake, *'hold still you little runt.'*

Blood dripped into the sink below him and trickled down to the plughole. Isaac dropped the blade and pulled at his open scar.

Deep within his mind, nobody spoke. Jack Ketch rolled the body of Ishmael into the grave then picked up his shovel. Mrs Punch fiddled with the end of Scaramouche's hat and looked at the grave next to Ishmaels where her lover laid in rest.

'We remember our friends,' said the blind man. 'We will remember them and miss them for the life they shared with us.'

The policeman opened his black book and drew the face of Pretty Polly with a tear under her eye.

'May they rest in peace with God,' said the blind man.

Mrs Punch stepped forward and dropped Scaramouche's hat onto his chest. Jack Ketch followed it with a shovel full of sand.

The Devil threw Ishmael's knife into the grave. It sliced into the ground by his side then disappeared as Mr Punch pushed some sand back into the hole.

Pretty Polly turned as Scaramouche's dog, Toby, dragged the unconscious body of Isaac from under the tent. He thrashed his head from side to side as he tugged at Isaac's trouser leg; a deep growl sounded over the graves.

The doctor pushed Toby away, stooped down and looked at the wet stain on Isaac's trousers.

'What's happening to him?' asked the Devil.

'Nothing that a few pills can't sort out,' said the doctor, taking a bottle of blue pills from his bag.

'Doctor, I saw Gabriel touch you,' said the Devil. 'What was it he said? Remember. Remember what?'

'Why should I tell you? Who appointed you as our leader?' said the doctor, looking at the label on the bottle.

The Devil leapt forward and shoved the doctor to the ground. The blue pills spewed out of the bottle and tumbled over the sand like little acrobats. The Devil pushed his foot into the doctor's stomach. The doctor winced. The Devil's eyes turned bright red.

'TELL ME.'

The sound from his words flew out in all directions. Some of it raced over the top of the gang and hit a rock face sat far back at the edge of the beach. The smooth curve of the sandstone amplified the sound as it reflected back. Other echoes returned from the smooth curved surface of the large waves crashing into shore …

-TELL ME – TELL ME – TELL ME-

'No,' said the doctor who had placed his hands over his ears, 'How do I know I can trust you?'

'That's not for you to decide,' said the Devil. 'You are going to tell me.'

'Okay okay,' said the doctor. 'Get your damn foot off me.'

The Devil lifted his boot and stood towering over the doctor. Isaac opened his eyes, then closed them again.

'Right. I … I … look can we all sit down,' said the doctor.

Pretty Polly put her hand on the doctor's shoulder.

'Are you all right? Do you want a cup of hot tea?'

The doctor hesitated then nodded. Polly disappeared into the striped tent.

'You may find it hard to understand what I am about to tell you,' said the doctor looking at the Devil.

'Just share with us everything Gabriel deposited into that wooden head of yours,' said the Devil.

'Okay.'

Isaac spat some sand from his mouth and started to crawl towards his gun lying in the sand next to Ishmael's grave.

The doctor took a deep breath. 'After Isaac was born his memories were fluid. At five, his brain constructed a permanent image into which he could store his memories. When he watched our show, although he was separated from his parents, his laughter overrode his sense of fear and he used this beach to form a 'happy place,' for his thoughts and experiences.'

Jack Ketch paused from shovelling sand over Ishmael and leant on his shovel to listen.

'How were the memories recalled?' said the Devil.

'They'd simply swim back out to sea,' said the doctor.

'A bit like sperm?' said Pretty Polly, returning from the tent.

The doctor looked at her.

'In a way, I suppose. Both hold information that is unlocked. Once in deep water, the bubbles forming the bodies of the memories fracture and revert back into sound waves. A single bubble then encapsulates the sound waves and carries them up to the surface. There it floats up into Isaac's consciousness.'

'So it is like sperm,' said Pretty Polly holding out a cup of tea to the doctor. 'They swim out and meet an egg.'

'I suppose you could think of a bubble being like an egg,' said the doctor looking surprised. 'Thank you,' he said taking the cup.

'Sugar?'

'No thanks,' said the doctor. He took a sip.

Isaac's hand reached out to his pistol.

'So what were we all doing in Gyrus?' said the Devil.

The doctor opened his mouth to answer, but turned at the shouts from Punch.

'That's the way to do it! That's the way to do it!'

'Damn it, Punch, shut up,' said the doctor.

The Devil looked over; Mr Punch was bringing his slapstick down over Isaac's head and singing: 'Killed by his own folly, killed by his own folly.'

'Get him off me,' said Isaac.

Blood started appearing from Isaac's scar.

'You murderer,' screamed Judy.

She launched herself at him, beating her fists into his chest and pushed him into Ishmael's grave.

The Devil stepped forward and put his hand on Judy's shoulder.

'Leave him be, Judy.'

Judy withdrew and sat sobbing in the sand. Pretty Polly brushed a wisp of hair from her face, then walked over to her.

'Cup of tea?'

Judy glanced up, 'Thank you.'

'Amazing what a nice cup of tea can do,' said the blind man. 'Sorts out any problem; brings things into perspective. Sort of binds us together in a common beverage.'

The Devil looked down at Isaac.

'So who do you think you are at the moment?'

Isaac pushed the dead body of Ishmael away from him and climbed out of the hole. Jack Ketch raised his shovel ready to strike.

'Isaac … my name is Isaac.'

'Good I'm glad you've sorted that out,' said the Devil.

'Actually you are a mental construct of Isaac,' said the doctor, 'inside his head.'

'I killed Gabriel and Ishmael,' said Isaac.

'And you killed my Scaramouche,' said Judy.

Isaac placed his head into his hands and fell silent. The gang looked at the Devil. The shovel in Jack Ketch's hand trembled, tea slurped over the rim of the cup in Polly's outstretched hand.

Isaac tried to hide in the darkness; images of bullets and death flowed in to torment him. Unable to escape the reality of his actions, he looked at the Devil.

'You aren't really the Devil are you?' said Isaac, backing away.

'No, I'm just a puppet like everyone else here.'

'Are you going to kill us all?' said Pretty Polly.

'No, I ... can I sit down?'

Mr Punch kicked Isaac's feet from under him and Isaac landed on the sand with a thump.

'Can I continue?' said the doctor. 'I think he should listen to what Gabriel told me.'

'Go on,' said the Devil.

'Well, the beach is a mental construct, however, there is another; it floats in the upper layers of Isaac's brain surrounded by neuron skyways. It is a place of darkness and weeping and fear.'

'HM Temporal Gyrus.' said the blind man.

'Damn right. Temporal Gyrus was a place created during the early embryonic development of Isaac. It is designed to hold unwholesome experiences and potentially damaging thoughts.'

'So why is the beach deserted apart from you lot?' said Isaac.

'You had a nervous breakdown, Isaac,' said the doctor. 'You couldn't face reality anymore after the car crash. In an attempt to return to a childhood innocence you besieged your happy place to take your memories. Many died; those who survived were enslaved along with the memory of the crash in Temporal Gyrus. There you formed custodians who acted as parent figures for you and allowed out only memories that didn't conflict with your delusion of safety and well being.'

'That's not true,' said Isaac. 'You're lying.'

'Why do I have no memory of all of this?' said Jack Ketch.

'The custodians suppressed the memory of the event in everyone,' said the doctor.

'So all new thoughts get sent directly to Temporal Gyrus now?' said Pretty Polly.

'Yes,' said the doctor.

'Rebekah?' said Isaac. 'Is Rebekah in there?'

The doctor placed his hand on Isaac's shoulder.

'Yes.'

'Jacob and Esau?'

The doctor nodded.

Isaac stared out over the waves.

'What have I done?'

A silence fell over the beach. The storm clouds over the sea moved in closer to shore. Thunderbolts and lightning continued to flash down far out over the water.

'I will stop this,' said Isaac. 'I shall go to Temporal Gyrus and rebalance things. I will release my family and return to the beach.'

'No that's impossible,' said the doctor. 'You will damn well fail at it. You do know that you have passed from your world don't you?'

'What?'

'You are dead Isaac. You die when you fall from the hospital window. You need to go to Rebekah and be reunited with her, not try and bring her memory back to life.'

'I don't know what the hell you're talking about,' said Isaac.

'Your wife and children do not live on in your mind,' continued the doctor, 'Rebekah is dead, so is Esau. So is Jacob really. You'd be interacting with yourself, animating your past memory of them in a way you believe they would act now. It is unreal. All of us here are only manipulations of past events by your mind. You are surrounded by yourself. You will be consigning yourself to a life of introspective hell.'

'I don't believe you,' said Isaac raising his voice. 'Goodbye everybody -'

'No,' interrupted the Devil. 'I will not let you go. Not until you find her again. Rebekah is waiting for you.'

A wave broke on the beach. It rang out the strike on a piano key …

Plink.

Plink, plink.

Plink, plink, plink.

'Go on, Isaac,' came the distorted voice of Fable over the sound.

Isaac got up and ran past the gang up the beach. The gang gave chase. Jack Ketch was the quickest. He overtook the Devil and followed Isaac's footprints through an archway in the red sandstone cliff.

There he stopped.

The rest of the gang caught up with him. A hush fell over them; a gorge was cut into the rock before them. The red sandstone that gave it its form bore down onto the pool of sand below, changing the granular yellow into a smooth orange hue. The mouth of the gorge was wide and vast. At the rear of the arena a narrow winding path threaded its way farther back into the rock.

The doctor looked at the contours of the rock streaming upwards into the sky. He took a step back out onto the beach.

'What is this place?'

He looked up at the archway. Within the contours of the weathered rock were faint words.

Ruined in a day.

'Ruined in a day?'

The doctor's words floated up to the rock face and bounced back. Flowing around him they trickled down into the sea. For a moment the beach became quiet as it reflected on the past. Then music lifted up on a wave of sorrow. It soared into the sky, swooped down over the gang's heads, and passed through the archway into the gorge.

Gaining speed inside, it started circling around; the acoustics of the hollow amplifying the sound. The doctor placed his hands over his ears and stepped back under the arch.

A large outcrop jutted out towards one side of the gorge. The music slammed against it each time it passed and scoured into it. A shower of red sand fell from the outcrop. It gathered together below and swelled into a river of flowing sand. The torrent raced towards the gang, flowed out through the archway and down the beach. The Punch and Judy puppets waded through the swirling sand around their feet and rushed to the side of the gorge. They stood watching as the river roared past them.

'What the hell did you do, doctor?' said the Devil.

'Damn if I know, I just read the words over the archway.'

'What words?' said the Devil.

The doctor leaned into the Devil and whispered, 'Ruined in a day.'

'What?' shouted the Devil back at him, unable to hear over the roar of sand and the boom of the music.

'Ruined in a day,' shouted the doctor.

The music paused then faded, the river of red slowed to a trickle. The notes withdrew back through the archway and splashed back into the sea. Polly started to cry, overwhelmed by the emotions stirred within.

Breathless, the rest of the gang fell to their knees. The doctor looked up to where the music had scoured at the rock.

'A face,' he cried. 'Look a face.'

The gang turned to where he had pointed and looked at the musical carving; it was the face of a woman.

'She is beautiful,' said the doctor.

'Who is she?' said Jack Ketch.

'Rebekah,' said Pretty Polly. 'The face of Rebekah.'

Fable appeared out of the darkness on the path at the back of the gorge. He walked towards Isaac. Isaac stood with thousands of mounds surrounded him. They followed the curve of the back wall in rows. Each mound had a wooden cross at the end of it.

'Who is it?' said Fable looking at one of the headstones.

Isaac glanced up; his eyes moist.

'It's one of the other children who watched the Punch and Judy show with me. I killed the other children. I killed them all.'

Fable held out Donaldson's mask and gun.

'Go back to Temporal Gyrus and redeem yourself.'

'Who are you?'

'A friend, take them.'

Isaac looked at the huge tinted lenses as the light continued to dim over the beach. His blue eyes twinkled then disappeared as he pulled on the face of black plastic. Isaac looked around with Donaldson's eyes. The small figures of the gang at the entrance to the gorge reflected in his black tinted glare. The curve of the gorge wrapped around them in the distortion of the image enclosing them within red walls.

'Yes, I shall restore this paradise,' said Isaac. 'I will make good the wrong I have done.'

'Good man.'

Isaac ran back through the gorge. The gang swept back at the sight of him, gun in hand. Isaac slowed towards the sea, hesitated for a moment, then splashed into the waves.

Chapter 16
You Will Hear of Wars

Abimelech swam up past the viewing window of the Subconscious Tavern. The sound of drunken singing flowed out and drifted down into the darkness. The custodian passed through the light beams cast from the outside lanterns and continued towards the surface. Above him two legs dangled awaiting ascension.

Abimelech circled a few times then reared up out of the water.

'Christ!' said Isaac, 'What the hell?'

Abimelech's pincers snapped around Isaac's head. Orbs squelched from the tips of his tentacles and span in the air. Isaac looked at it through the mask of Donaldson, his breathing heavy through the filter at the side of his face.

'This is not going to help,' said Abimelech. 'You must be shielded from the pain of this world, I cannot allow you to rape and pillage Isaac's memories.'

'No,' shouted Isaac, 'Rebekah is my wife; I will not allow her to stay locked away under your tyranny.'

Abimelech plunged his tentacles into the water and grabbed Isaac's feet.

'You are Donaldson,' said Abimelech. 'You have no wife, you have become deluded, let me help you.'

Isaac reached for his gun. One arm kept him steady in the water. The other raised his semi-automatic pistol. Drops of water fell from its barrel. The reflection of Abimelech wrapped itself around his dark lenses.

Drip, drip, drip.

BLAM. BLAM. BLAM.

Three bullet shells span up into the air.

Three bullets raced towards the custodian.

Two approached the tentacles thrashing in the air. The third cut through Isaac's mind towards Abimelech's head. The reflection of the bullets grew smaller on the surface of the water as they gained height.

'Stop,' said Abimelech.

The three bullets froze in front of the custodian.

'You can't kill me, Tom.'

'Let Rebekah go.'

'No.'

The custodian pulled Isaac into the air.

'Donaldson, you are my creation, my first born. I fashioned you to help Isaac play out his boyhood fantasies in his mind. You were part of the system of regression back to a time of naiveté and happiness that Isaac had before Rebekah's blood was shed.'

'I .. I am Isaac.'

'No,' said Abimelech, 'You are Tom Donaldson, you are to protect Isaac, honour and obey me, Tom, in that you will serve Isaac well. Persist in this delusion and you will bring him great harm.'

The orbs encircled Isaac in a large donut formation. As they closed in, they seemed to change and become one moving body. Isaac saw an image like a leopard form; seven heads writhed at the end of its neck. Each moved as a snake towards him until seven sets of black and white teeth filled his vision.

'I am ...' said Isaac, 'I am ... Donaldson.'

'Good, good,' said Abimelech. 'Now, Tom, even as we speak a battalion of sentries storm the beach to rid Isaac of the renegade Punch and Judy gang. Go now and make sure that none survive.'

On the beach the gang watched as the sentries walked out of the sea. Shaking the water from their long white hair, the old men broke from formation and moved out to form long lines stretching out along the shoreline. With a clicking of old bones they brought their muskets down in unison and started to march. The gang stood willing their feet to carry them to safety; their breath forming bubbles in the air from their open mouths. A blue wave crashed onto the shore throwing a cloud of white over the army.

Mrs Punch held her baby close to her chest and soothed him with her voice.

'There're just old men,' said Polly, 'just old men.'

The Devil pushed past her and strode forward. He hesitated as he felt a hand on his shoulder.

'Don't,' said the doctor.

The Devil looked at him for a moment. Then placed his hand on the doctor's shoulder.

'Someone's got to sort this mess out.'

The Devil stepped forward, pushed his shoulders back, and appeared to double in size.

'Get the hell off our beach.'

The echoes from his voice bounced around the sentries. The authority in the words compelled a response. Some of the sentries turned and headed back into the sea. The rest seemed to be considering the same journey. The gang behind the Devil started to think about following them. The Devil glanced back as he heard the shuffle of their feet behind him.

'No not you lot!'

The gang checked themselves and held firm. The Devil's instructions bounced off the rock at the back of the beach, streamed over his head and hit the sentries ...

'No not you lot!'

Released from the previous command, the sentries brought the flints down on their muskets. Sparks flew into the air as firecrackers around them, lead balls shot out of the long muzzles.

The baby began to cry as lead perforated the tent. The Devil stepped back, a hole smouldering in his shoulder.

'Shh,' said Mrs Punch to the baby. 'I won't let you die.'

The sentries unclipped powder bags from their replaced hips and poured powder down the muzzles of their muskets.

'What are you doing?' said Polly to the blind man, who was digging around her feet.

'I mined the beach front with memories Isaac had of his father to try to stop the custodians invasion last year,' said the blind man. 'We can use them as weapons.'

'Right,' said Polly, 'Toby, dig.'

Toby sniffed the sand then started digging. A moment later an Old Spice bottle bobbed up out of the sand. Then another and another.

The blind man picked one up as the sentries tapped wooden rods down onto their powder. He weighed the bottle in his hand as lead balls fell through smooth wood towards powder beds; he pulled the stopper out with his teeth and looked up at the sound of wadding being rammed down. The rest of the gang scooped up more Old Spice bottles appearing around them.

'Take aim,' said a sentry.

The blind man stepped up, 'Our weapons are not the weapons of your world, they have divine power to demolish the likes of you.' A volley of spit followed his words. In unison the gang pulled their hands back.

'Fire!' said the sentry.

'Fire!' said the blind man.

A volley of Old Spice bottles sailed up into the air. Musket balls whizzed around the gang, one clipped the top of Mrs Punch's mobcap, the rest fell into the sand. The Old Spice bottles reached the top of their arcs and fell down around the ancient army. Each one in turn delivered its message in the voice of Isaac's father...

'Eat your peas. How can you have any pudding if you don't finish your peas?'

'You're not going out without a coat are you?'

'Finish your dinner before getting down.'

'Have you done your homework?'

The sentries paused as they listened, laughed and started to reload again.

'It's not working,' said Polly.

'I don't think we are using them in context,' said Mrs Punch.

'What are we going to do now?' said Jack Ketch.

'I haven't a clue,' said the blind man, 'I guess this is it.'

Polly looked at Punch who was tapping his slapstick across his open hand.

'A clue?' said Polly, 'A clue - come on, Punch, 'I'm going to need your help.'

Polly span around in the sand and taking Punch by the hand led him into the tent.

Inside, Polly searched around, 'Find me some newspaper, Punch.'

'What? Aren't we going to-'

'Are you mad? We are under attack, I haven't brought you in here for sex.'

'O.'

'Newspaper, Punch,' said Polly as she whipped her bra and knickers off. 'Use the fish and chip wrapping in the corner.'

'Now I'm confused,' said Mr Punch looking at Polly's naked body.

'Shut up and wrap it over me.'

'Okay,' said Mr Punch, 'whatever turns you on, Pol.'

Punch secured the newspaper and stepped back.

'Sexy, but smelly,' he said as the stink of fish and chips wafted over him. 'Now what?'

'Something I learnt at Gyrus, come on.'

Punch followed Polly out of the tent; his hands over his groin.

'What on earth?' said Judy.

Polly walked down the beach towards the sentries. Seeing her they stopped and stared, their old fingers reaching for their crossword pencils behind hair filled ears. They moved to the side and allowed Polly amongst them.

'Sorry boys, no crossword today,' said Polly. 'But the headlines are worth a look.'

The sentries looked at the large print across Polly's breasts; a chorus of soft thuds surrounded her as their muskets dropped to the sand.

'Come on, don't be shy.'

'This is absolutely disgusting,' said Mrs Punch.

Polly got down on the sand, put her hands behind her head and pushed her chest up. The sentries settled down around her and started to read. Mr Punch walked towards them smiling.

'Nash out for a duck,' said a sentry.

'My shares are up,' said another.

'That's the only thing that is-'

The sentry fell silent into the sand. Punch grinned and moved around whacking his slapstick across rows of heads singing, 'That's the way to do it, that's the way to do it!'

Behind the gang, Fable walked over to Ishmael's grave and held his hand over it. The sand shifted, bulged, the handle of a blade appeared. Fable smiled as the knife floated up out of the mound into his hand. Jack Ketch glanced back at the sound, yet saw nothing. He returned his gaze to Punch and Polly as the sentries continued to fall.

When Punch had finished, Polly got up and looked at the dead bodies around her.

'That, you old perverts, is for my friends at Gyrus that you prostitute with your cryptic clues and your fallen todgers.'

Mr Punch beamed back at the rest of the gang, 'Wow, Poll's hot!'

'Shut up, Punch,' said Polly.

'Can we?' said Punch.

'No,' said Polly and walked back towards the tent, the smell of fish and chips following her.

Chapter 17
The Temptation of Isaac

The black horse kicked hooves into the yellow sky; its long mane flowing north across southern plains. It stopped as a red light flared up before it and receded back onto the bonnet of Ishmael's F355 Ferrari. A young boy stepped out and started to wipe it down.

'No thanks,' said Ishmael.

The boy looked up and hesitated. The rear view mirror cast a dark shadow across Ishmael's eyes.

'Nice mask,' said the boy.

'I'm sorry?' said Ishmael.

Ishmael gripped the wheel with his black leather gloves.

'Where's Tonto?' said the boy.

The traffic lights turned amber.

'Look get lost kid.'

Ishmael pushed his foot down on the accelerator. The boy whacked the back of the car with the flat of his hand as it passed by.

'Hi ho Silver, away.'

In the hospital, Isaac washed his blood from the sink. The voice in his head of Mr Punch had been cut out, to be replaced by the image of breasts cupped in peach satin. He watched them holding their curves as Polly cornered in the sand.

Isaac took his hand away from his open scar. The bleeding had stopped. Blood caked fingers turned the tap that washed his pain into the past. He walked out of the bathroom leaving a trail of urine footprints on the floor.

Poking his head around the door, he searched around for Gabriel. No sign. Isaac stumbled out to look for him, images playing in his mind of Gabriel dying, until the walls of the corridor receded as if water and Isaac shuffled forward, his mind unconnected with his surroundings. Buffeted by the spirit of commerce, he turned with the stream of people and a hungry stomach into the hospital shopping mall.

The noise confused him and became the chatter of the Punch and Judy gang. Isaac placed his hands over his ears. He looked up, the mall became a desert of sand, the people a restless sea.

Isaac walked up to a large tent on the beach. Children, that Isaac saw as spectres of the dead swirling around the tethers to the tent, shovelled sweets at the pick-and-mix in the reality of the hospital shop. Inside the tent, Isaac found a small kitchen. Pretty Polly looked up from washing the dishes and shrank back, 'Are you going to kill me now?'

Isaac passed her without turning. He pushed open a door and entered a supermarket hidden in the expanding space of the fabric. Looking around he saw a fallen stack of baked bean cans: one lay off to the side crushed, covered in blood and surrounded by packets of lentils.

'Something has happened, something bad,' thought Isaac. He walked over to a row of magazines sat on the top shelf above the daily papers. Isaac stooped down and read the black and white headlines …

Woman Killed by Supermarket Sociopath.

'Mum?'

Images of calico curtains swayed around the baked bean cans.

'Mum?'

Isaac looked up at the advertising monitor suspended from the ceiling. It showed his bedroom curtains, his mother, Sarah lying on the floor of a supermarket, Isaac standing over her crying. The man in the tatty red and black cloak kicked her with his black boots.

'No, Fable, please,' screamed Sarah.

'Matilda Mother!' said the man as he smashed a can of low salt baked beans into her face.

Isaac watched the flickering loop over:

-No, Fable, please, Matilda Mother! No, Fable, please, Matilda Mother-

Isaac looked away. Behind him he could hear the sound of laughter as the produce on the shelves started to shake, a bored voice called, *supervisor to the disturbance in aisle four please*, a packet of nacho crisps burst, cigarette packets shot filter tipped torpedoes into a stack of vitamin pills, gold tops flipped off milk bottles and flew into the air.

Isaac peered up through the golden rain and calmed himself; the shaking stopped. Milk flowed around his feet and mixed with the blood pooled around the baked bean can and the packets of lentil soup. Behind him he could hear footsteps. Fable stood looking at him.

'Hello, Isaac.'

'You ... you're the man in my dream.'

'Very perceptive, now-'

'You murdered the memory of my mother.'

Fable raised his hand, 'Shh now, Isaac, that was only a nightmare sent to scare you, I'm your friend ... Good, that's better, now, Isaac look above the newspapers again.'

'What?'

'All that you see, I give to you, Isaac, take enjoy.'

Isaac looked above the papers to the magazines. A copy of the Spotters Guide to Seagulls sat beside a House Beautiful magazine, tucked behind that was a copy of Playmate Search celebrating its 50th anniversary of Playmates. It had Rebekah on its cover, wisps of hair obscuring her nipples to strip her of indecent exposure. Isaac picked it up, thumbed through the pages and stopped at a picture of Rebekah lying face down on the beach, her bikini undone; the side of her breast visible, sand across the curve of her bottom.

'Excuse me, sir, are you going to buy that?'

The supermarket within the tent receded; the reality of the hospital mall folded in around him, a manila envelope over forbidden letters. Isaac turned, the shopkeeper stood before him.

'Er, no … why would people want to buy this in a hospital?'

'Are you going to buy it?'

Isaac fumbled for his pocket and remembered he was in his gown. He had no money.

A woman bumped into the back of him; Isaac fell forward and returned to the beach.

'Daddy, Daddy!'

Isaac looked around; he was back in the supermarket within the tent, a voice of a small child fluttering like a butterfly against his cheek. The butterfly lifted up and flew down aisle four. Isaac followed, searching. Delicate wings took him past Pretty Polly again and back through the flaps of the tent. Isaac looked down the beach; the butterfly lifted into the air. Jacob was running towards him.

'Jacob!'

Isaac ran down the beach towards his son and embraced him.

'Jacob, you've woken up, thank God!'

Isaac felt a tap on his shoulder and turned.

'You'll have to come with me, sir,' said the shopkeeper.

Isaac stood outside the newsagent in the hospital mall, a daily paper and a Playmate magazine, with Roxanne Siordia on the cover, in his hands.

'No, no.'

Isaac searched for Jacob.

'Come on,' said the shopkeeper. 'I'm going to have to call security.'

'But,' said Isaac, 'It was a mistake, I thought I saw my son.'

'Your son?'

'Jacob, he's six. He was standing right here.'

The shopkeeper examined Isaac, 'There was no child here, sir.' He noticed the blood under Isaac's eye and added, 'which ward are you on?'

Isaac felt giddy, disorientated.

'Where am I?'

'Listen,' said the shopkeeper, 'You clearly shouldn't be here, give me those and I'll get someone to take you back to your room.'

Isaac ripped the cover off the Playmate Search and handed the mutilated magazine and paper over.

'Can I keep this?' he said holding the cover to his chest.

'You madman ... no ... look don't push your luck, give it to me.'

A small crowd of people gathered, as Isaac tried to stop the shopkeeper from taking the torn cover. There was a tug, a struggle, then a ripping noise as a tear snaked down Roxanne Siordia.

'Christ,' said Isaac, 'Rebekah ... you've ruined her picture.'

'What did he say?' said a man in the crowd.

'I think I'm going to be sick,' said Isaac; he bent over and vomited over the feet of the shoppers.

Isaac woke. He lay in a pull out bed beside his son, a pillow behind his head. Before him the image of Rebekah pressed into the room. She hung suspended with her hands and feet bleeding out from her as if plastic mould from an air-fix kit. The curtains behind her flipped off their runners and swept through her towards him. He invited them in and let them flow down his throat to choke the growl that struggled to give voice to his despair.

The image receded and Deborah stood before him.

'Sit up.'

Isaac looked at her and groaned. Deborah plumped the pillows.

'I heard you stole a paper and a Playboy from the shop.'

'I ... er.'

'Look, Mr Steward, you passed out, you're obviously suffering from stress, don't concern yourself with what happened.'

Isaac fell back onto his pillow.

'Thank you.'

157

Deborah smiled, 'I believe you wanted this.'

She handed Isaac the cover of the Playmate; a piece of tape held it together.

'Thanks,' said Isaac. 'About earlier.'

'Yes?'

'I'm sorry if I embarrassed you. You must think I'm some kind of-'

'Shh, Mr Steward, I think nothing of the sort. I've seen you with your son, you are a good man.'

'Thank you,' said Isaac. 'It's been an upsetting day.'

'I'm sorry to hear that.'

Isaac touched his finger to the plaster under his eye.

'It shouldn't need stitches,' said Deborah. 'I cleaned it up as best I could.'

'I -'

'It doesn't matter,' said Deborah. 'You should talk to someone about it though.'

Isaac's mobile started to ring. Deborah raised an eyebrow. Isaac glanced at the display: *Jane Peter.*

'Sorry,' said Isaac, 'I forgot to turn it off.'

Deborah smiled and pulled her mobile from her pocket. She turned the display, its wallpaper a picture of her black cat, and showed it to Isaac.

'Still on as well.'

The ringing stopped.

'It doesn't really effect the equipment,' said Deborah. 'It will drop your sperm count though.'

Isaac looked at Deborah, then at his phone. Deborah turned her mobile off and turned the black screen towards him. Isaac could feel a tingle running down the back of his spine. He pressed the red button on his phone, the electronic connection to its power severed and it went dead.

'There it's off,' said Isaac showing Deborah.

Deborah continued to show him her blank screen. Isaac's hand trembled, the two mobiles connecting them for a moment.

'I think I'm unravelling,' said Isaac breaking the silence, 'I saw Jacob in the mall.'

'You're just tired. Get some rest, I'll be back in an hour to see if you're well enough to go home.'

'Can't you stay? I feel I can talk to you.'

'I have patients to tend to, we could chat later if you like.'

'Okay,' said Isaac and rolled over onto his side. Sweat started to drip from his forehead onto the pillow.

Deborah walked to the door, glanced back over her shoulder at Isaac, then disappeared into the hospital machine.

An hour passed.

Isaac got to his feet, peeled back a notice on the wall warning that physical assaults on NHS staff will lead to prosecution, and taking some Blu-Tack applied it to the Playmate cover. He placed it next to the NHS sign and stood back.

'I love you, Rebekah. I won't let them hurt you again.'

He turned and looked at his son.

'Please wake up, Jacob.'

Sighing, Isaac turned to walk towards the window. As he did, he banged his leg against Jacob's bed. The metal framework shook. The bed made a creaking sound and nudged up against Jacob's bedside table. The chipboard under its cheap laminate shifted and Jacob's figurine lost its footing. Buzz Lightyear fell face first towards the hard floor. The coffee cup followed and splashed around him. Isaac paused for a moment as images of Ishmael falling on the beach filled his mind.

He turned to stare up at the moon; thoughts of Rebekah under the Dandelion Tree traced around the curve of its reflected light.

'Rebekah,' he whispered through lips that remembered her kisses as wine.

Her name repeated in his mind blocking out all other thoughts, and when he tired, he took it and recycled it: stretching, mashing and pulping he multiplied and divided. Looking out at the light touching the top of the trees, he delivered the newly formed thought to the pane before him.

'I want to see Rebekah again. I want my Little Bear back.'

Tears flowed down his cheeks as he spoke. Probabilities collapsed before him to form a dark tunnel; he walked through to the window. Reaching out his hand, he placed it against the glass. The pads at the tips of his fingers turned blue from its touch. Isaac pushed up the window and looked down onto the pavement below.

In the distance Isaac heard the siren of a police car searching for judgement. Isaac's freedom dined on his sensibilities which disappeared behind his rib cage. He felt nothing; a white-out of emotional withdrawal. He stepped through the window and balanced on the ledge outside. Behind him he heard his row of dominoes ...

CLINK. CLINK. CLINK.

The dominoes ran under his feet and up to the edge of the ledge. The last one, a double six, resisted the push of the domino before it then succumbed to fate. It toppled off the edge and span in a blur of black and white towards the ground. Isaac watched it hit the tarmac. It bounced upward, clinked one last time against the hard stone of the hospital steps then sank into the car-park.

Silence.

'That's it then,' thought Isaac. 'I have no choice but to follow.'

The edge of Isaac's green gown billowed in the wind as he struggled to find a secure footing. As he did, flecks of rust fell from the contorted railings running along the front of the ledge. Isaac stared ahead.

'Don't look down. Don't look down.'

Tiny drops of rain started to spit down from the sky. They tapped around the glass above him.

Plink.

Plink, plink.

Plink, plink, plink.

Isaac looked straight ahead and heard the distorted voice of Fable, 'Go on, Isaac.'

A flock of magpies broke away from circling overhead. They swooped down towards Isaac. The birds stopped in front of his face and beat down on him with their black wings. Isaac's world went black and white. He felt dizzy. The birds screamed at him. Their harsh and aggressive -Chak-Chak-Chak- made his head hurt. The sound distorted and became the distant voice of Fable in his mind. He barely heard it over the noise of the beating wings.

'Throw yourself down from here,' said Fable, 'For surely your God will command his angels to save you.'

Isaac placed his hands over his ears.

Rebekah, Isaac, Jacob, Esau.

Rebekah, Isaac, Jacob, Esau.

The blackness withdrew into orange and black stripes. The birds flew over to a large willow tree and watched. Isaac fell silent, turning he looked at Jacob. The heart monitor inside continued to follow the rhythm of his life beat.

BEEP ... 'I can't live with the pain, Jacob.'

BEEP ... 'I'm going home now, back to your mother.'

BEEP.

The last beep seeped away into the walls; the green trace of the heart monitor recorded a flat line for a second as Jacob's heart missed a beat.

BEEP.

BEEP.

'You are dead, Isaac. You die when you fall from the hospital window.'

Isaac turned away, unable to look at his son. He flattened his hands against the stone, and as an oar against an iron clad sca his mind pulled across sinew and bone to move him through the strange waters. Trembling, he started to take a step forward. Sweat poured down his forehead. He placed his foot back on the ledge. His body started shaking. Isaac swayed backwards and forwards. A pressure to jump; to delay no longer overwhelmed him, the need to ejaculate despite the desire to withhold. Isaac's body rocked to the point of no return. He felt heavy as if a stone falling through water to the bed below. Closing his eyes, he stepped off.

His body snapped and pulped as it hit.

Darkness flowed into his mouth finding the hollows inside.

Choking. Darkness.

The never ending darkness.

A spot of light appeared at the edge of Isaac's mind. He felt flesh wrap itself around bones, warmth, nerves tingling. The light increased until unable to stand the glare he opened his eyes. Before him loomed the wall of the hospital. He reached out, it felt cold, yet he could sense warmth buried deep below. Bricks shifted as he prepared to climb for a second time. The wall tried to find the form to fit the impression of skin pressed against it. Isaac looked out across the car-park and waited until he was sure that the wall and he had become one. A hollow formed; Isaac pressed his hand in and blurred the boundary between flesh and brick.

The winter sun played with the canvas below finding its way into nooks and crannies; moss and hollows; painting a yellow hue that was insipid; the promise of warmth withheld until the earth tipped a nod to its God. Clouds swept over the top of the hospital. Isaac watched a magpie glide on the thermals then pulled up on his handhold and set his toes against the smooth face.

A wind crept around from the north and flowed either side of Isaac, outlining his shape in movement. Isaac stopped and felt it against his cheeks. Forming solid edges to his hand again, he found definition in his blue tipped fingers and raised his head. He could smell pollen, bluebells against water, snowdrops through snow. Images of movement came with the wind: children, trains, butterflies, boots revealing grit under virgin snow.

Isaac swept aside the memories and focused again on being still so that he could see in his mind's eye the position of the window. He slowed his breathing and saw himself falling. Isaac blinked and looked around: the order of the open space calmed him and he pushed his fear into the ends of his toes.

Isaac looked up, the clouds above grew darker, the wind left him, the smell of promised spring left his nostrils, the magpie became two, then three, then one continuous circle of flight.

And then in the stillness, high above, just to the right, Isaac saw the window.

Isaac felt his insides become fluid. Everything seemed transient to him, nothing within was still, his organs became water, his bones white froth on blood.

He set out and the wall itself became fluid as Isaac swam through towards his son. Gravity span in confusion and tugged one way, then another. The brick kept him close, embracing Isaac in its form, protecting him from the consequence of separation. At points Isaac's body seemed to sink into the wall, but he kept his eyes ever on the end before him.

Isaac surfaced just below the window that he had leapt from moments ago. Rust fell as orange rain from the contorted railings running along the front of the ledge. Isaac looked as the magpie swooped down and perched on it. It turned its head, met his eyes then flew off again. Isaac's pulse increased; his hand now clammy.

He looked down at the noise of a car. Below him was his body, an arm pocking up from the concrete. It sank leaving five small indentations in the ground as a blue Ferrari pulled into the car park. Ishmael got out and stood beneath Isaac.

'Isaac!'

Isaac opened his eyes and went stiff at the sound of his brother.

'Shit,' he said and pulled himself over the ledge and through the open window.

Chapter 18
Forgive Your Brother

A crack raced up the glass of the window at Isaac's first blow. His second attempt succeeded and his fist passed through. His wrists followed passing close to thirsty shards.

'Bloody Ishmael,' shouted Isaac.

Lines radiated out from his strike, jagging their way to the safety of the wooden frame. As he withdrew his arm, two sharp spines of glass stuck into his hand. He looked up at the moon through the hole in the glass, as a drop of blood pooled then dropped onto the floor.

'Bloody Ishmael.'

A wind picked up and flowed through bringing with it the scent of peach blossom from the trees. The smell brought back images of the Clown Loach spinning in the toilet under the flow of his bladder. Isaac sat down and gripped the side of the chair. Beside him Jacob's television monitor played Mary Poppins. Isaac turned and watched her descending on her umbrella; grinding his eyes into his hands, he started rocking in the chair.

'What to do? What to do?'

Isaac tried to think through the chemical wash rising within him.

'Run or fight?'

Isaac's pupils dilated. Adrenaline jerked him between the predetermined responses to the approaching threat. He looked at the naked picture of Roxanne on the wall.

'Fight, Rebekah would have wanted me to fight.'

A flurry of cold comments drifted through his mind like snow. They cut Ishmael down before him.

The strike of shoes against the corridor floor raised Isaac's eyes. His heart tried to burrow out through his chest, a gestating parasite seeking release.

The handle turned and Ishmael stepped into the room; sand flew up on the beach within Isaac's mind, Ishmael shot up in a streak of yellow in a regenerated fifty-year-old body. He spoke to Isaac, forming new words to replace old memories, 'Hello, Isaac.'

'Fuck off.'

Ishmael touched the skin under his own eye.

'Plaster?'

'Leave now,' said Isaac.

'Listen-' started Ishmael.

'Fuck off,' interrupted Isaac.

Isaac looked at him as hatred for his brother erupted out as if spines of a porcupine.

'Isaac, we need to talk,' said Ishmael. 'You have died-'

'Fuck off.'

Isaac saw Ishmael's gaze turn to Jacob; he stepped in between them and pushed Ishmael backwards.

'Get your hands off me,' said Ishmael.

'Haven't I made myself clear?' said Isaac. 'Go fuck yourself.'

'For Christ sakes, Isaac,' said Ishmael. 'Let me speak.'

'Listen, you half-blood outcast,' said Isaac. 'No one wants you, don't you get it?'

'I ...' Ishmael resisted with stilted words that protruded from his mouth; his resolve faltered, '... you uncircumcised wanker, Isaac.'

The words stung Isaac as crushed chillies across eyes.

The brothers sank through the hospital floor. A battle of hot words firing lead. Like Spitfires and Messerschmitts they circled each other above metal framed destroyers afloat on a sea of cut flowers. Blows started, awkward, the stop-motion affray on Argonauts. They passed an old man hobbling against arthritic joints. Quotes of derision marked them as they descended down through the valley of death in the A&E department; defibrillators charging to the left, charging to the right. Like coming over Pearl Harbour unannounced, they attacked above the waiting area, people looking around as they sank into plastic seats. Concrete foundations cracked as they exchanged parenthetic punches. The soil below choked them with worms boring through expletives to sanitise their disunity. They fell silent, as death and decay scuttled around them. Ishmael struggled to breathe. Finally with great effort he gasped, '... ruined in a day.'

Ishmael receded and in his mind's eye Isaac saw himself moving over a blue ocean towards a yellow beach far off in the distance. He soared up on the crest of a wave, dropped down and flew low over the beach. A large cliff face loomed up before him. He entered through an archway and circled around a gorge concealed behind it. Looking up he saw the image of Rebekah cut into the soft rock.

'She is waiting for you,' said Ishmael.

He grasped Isaac's hand and they ascended back to Jacob's room.

Isaac glared at Ishmael.

'How did you do that?'

'Gabriel told me the words to unlock the image.'

'Gabriel?'

'Isaac, let me take you to her.'

'I'm dead?' said Isaac.

Ishmael noticed the cover of the Playmate stuck to the wall with the tape running down it. He shook his head and said, 'You're clinically dead in about 7 minutes. You've been reliving your day, you're in danger of becoming lost in yourself.'

'I was able to go to them – they sang happy Birthday to me.'

'The first day of the rest of your life, Isaac.'

'But Jacob was there?' said Isaac, 'He's still alive, how could he be there?'

'He only has a short time left, Isaac.'

'No – I didn't leave him to die – you are lying – what the fuck am I talking to you for anyway?'

'Isaac, need we always be against each other?'

'Have you forgotten the river of excrement flowing between us?' said Isaac.

'We can make the decision to let go of the past,' said Ishmael. 'We can forgive each other and cast off the hate.'

'And I guess you hold me and my family responsible for that hate?' said Isaac.

'No. I accept responsibility for my actions. Now before it is too late, take my hand.'

'O for God's sake,' said Isaac, 'shut up.'

Ishmael extended his hand.

Isaac looked at it and shoved his hands into his pockets.

The memory of Ishmael and Donaldson on the beach rose in his mind. *'When does it stop, Isaac?'* sounded the words of Gabriel and for a moment Isaac glimpsed the futility of transient attrition as Ishmael fell backwards, slain by his hand, a bullet hole through his neck.

'Please, Isaac,' said Ishmael. 'I'm sorry, forgive me.'

Ishmael's words floated across towards Isaac. Silence fell over the room. Isaac became aware of a low-pitched note sounding in his ears. It reminded him of the drone of a disconnected call. The atmosphere became tense and pulled at the image in Isaac's mind of Ishmael's words until the 'me' in them became thin and transparent. The word 'forgive' remained and resonated around Isaac's head, trying to find a connection to replace the broken tone. Isaac tried to resist; the pain in his body numbed his pride. He extended his hand and connected with Ishmael. An audible click sounded as they shook and embraced each other.

'I forgive,' said Isaac. 'Forgive me for looking down on you.'

Ishmael patted Isaac's back, 'I do.'

The two figures stood in the embrace. Two semi-circles of horses with chariots of fire gathered unseen around them. Both ranks stretched back through the walls into the corridor and the wards beyond. They reared up in unison and snorted fire from their nostrils.

Ishmael stood back and looked at Isaac.

'Come with me to the Dandelion Tree – she is there.'

'I need to get dressed,' said Isaac.

Ishmael grabbed Isaac by the shoulders. The tendons on the back of his hands popped up to form white lines of tension.

'Listen, Isaac, you must come now. Do you understand? Now!'

Isaac looked at Ishmael and surrendered, 'Okay.'

The two brothers headed towards the door. Isaac hesitated and looked at Jacob. Then stepping back he placed his hand on Jacob's brow.

'Don't die, Jacob – it's not time to follow me, live your own life.'

Isaac turned and walked with Ishmael past the parading clowns, the shuffle of his feet in step with the click of Ishmael's shoes against the floor. Isaac looked up as he passed a room with its door open; inside Deborah was plumping a pillow and talking to an old man.

'Nearly at the lift,' said Ishmael.

Isaac leant against his brother for support, his failing strength resisting the movement away from the hospital where it felt at home amongst the sick.

'Can you hear a clinking sound?' said Isaac.

'No.'

'Hmm.'

The lift doors opened. The brothers walked in and stood in silence as the circle of lights on the lift panel indicated their descent past wards of metal framed beds and cut flowers. The lift stopped at the first floor and an old man with Argonaut arthritis hobbled in. He stared at Isaac as the doors closed behind, smiled and jabbed towards the ground floor button with his walking stick. Ishmael leant over and pressed it for him.

The lift stopped and opened at the A&E department. Isaac and Ishmael waited for the old man to exit, then made their way down the hall.

Behind plastic doors, Isaac could hear the sound of a crash team.

The fall has shattered his pelvis … wait he's going into ventricular fibrillation … Charging … Stand clear.'

Isaac stopped.

'Is that me in there?'

'Don't look, Isaac.'

'Charging … Stand clear.'

'I thought I could never die,' said Isaac, 'that I would go on forever.'

'You will, Isaac, just not in that body, it's fucked.'

'Time of death - seventeen hundred hours.'

Ishmael pushed through the double doors and entered the waiting area, a porter looked at them as they passed by. People sat deep in plastic seats looking at the triage nurse talking to an ambulance paramedic. Ishmael pulled at Isaac.

'Come on, before someone notices us.'

Outside they followed the worn track in the large stone steps down towards the car park. Ishmael searched around for his car.

'Where did I leave it?'

'It's there.' Isaac pointed to the Ferrari spider parked at an angle across two parking spaces.

Ishmael walked towards the pay machine and inserted his ticket into the highwayman. The parking fee flashed up on its display in green letters.

'Daylight robbery,' said Ishmael. 'They might as well employ someone to stick a gun at my head and shout – stand and deliver.'

Isaac followed Ishmael to his car; he winced as he got in.

Ishmael turned on the ignition. The V8 engine roared into life. Isaac sat looking ahead, still dressed in his hospital gown.

'I think I've gone mad,' he said finally. 'I can't think clearly anymore.'

'Gabriel told me I needed to get you to the Dandelion Tree before sundown today to save you,' said Ishmael.

'Ha – so it's come to this,' said Isaac. 'I have descended into the lunacy of fables and Cinderella clocks.'

'A moment ago you went into free fall into the tarmac.'

'And your point is?'

'You are in love, Isaac, it has a certain insanity.'

'Well,' said Isaac, 'I think perhaps this is some kind of dying flashback and that in a moment everything will blink into oblivion.'

Ishmael put his foot on the accelerator; the car surged forward and streaked away from the spectre of the hospital in a flash of azure blue. Isaac stared out at the world as it raced by him.

The Ferrari slowed and stopped at a red light.

'By the way,' said Ishmael, 'what was with the Playmate picture on the wall?'

Isaac turned and looked at the yellow giants in the demolition site next to the road. They ate the side of the building; metal girders and wires between their blunt teeth.

'Do you think it is appropriate to have that sort of thing in your son's room?'

'It is a picture of his Mum, of course it's bloody appropriate.'

'No, Isaac, it's a picture of a naked model.'

'And you point is?' said Isaac.

The lights changed to green.

Ishmael sighed. Isaac looked back at the row of giants who carried on oblivious to the passing of the brothers. He turned away as the image receded into his memory. In front of him he saw the black horse on the bonnet of Ishmael's car cutting through the flow of air racing over it.

As it sped onward the darkness of its skin lightened to become as white as snow. Isaac watched it as it reared up off the bonnet and raced ahead of the car. It charged before them full of hope and promise. A hint of a smile crossed Isaac's grey face as he rode off, the dying sun lighting the white horse dancing before him.

Chapter 19
The Tune of the Charmer

The red, white, and blue, bunting flags flapped in the breeze. Two old loudspeakers sat above them perched on each corner of the tent like two dishevelled parrots. The first tried to squawk *Pretty Polly*, but managed only static. The other responded with a crackle and pop. The speakers looked out over the sea and watched bubbles spin up into the air on the crests of waves, then with a loud screech of feedback, they burst into life.

The sound of Pretty Polly's singing floated out from them and drifted along the beach. The speakers lifted triumphantly up into the air. With a TWANG they both stopped with a jolt. They bobbed about looking at the expanse of sky above them. Each with a wire tethered to the tent below.

Inside the tent, Polly stood at the sink washing up the coffee mugs. She looked across at the hundreds of dirty cups left on the worktop and continued to sing. Hearing a noise, she glanced up. Brushing her hands down her apron to dry them she walked towards the secret supermarket in the back of the tent to investigate. A figure stood in the shadows of the open doorway.

'Hello Isaac?'

Fable stepped into the kitchen.

'Hello, Polly, quite the hero out there. Bravo.'

'Who are you?'

'Fable.'

'Who? '

'Corporal Clegg! Does no one remember me?'

Fable walked to the sink and grabbed a tea towel.

'Let me help, Polly.'

Polly stepped back towards the copper sink, 'I think I'd like you to leave.'

'How many sentries did you know on a professional basis at Gyrus?'

Polly looked at him.

'Go away.'

'Not just yet,' said Fable, 'I'd like to see what's behind the headlines.'

'What?'

'Your tease on the beach,' said Fable.

Fable took a step back and twirled his tea towel in the air. He grabbed the free end and held it tight between his hands. Stepping forward, he looped the tea towel over Polly's head, pulled her towards him, kissed her.

'Get off.'

Fable moved a hand down to one of her breasts and felt the firmness of the wood under her apron.

'O yes, did you like the touch of their old fingers scribbling the answers to their mind games over these curves in Gyrus?'

Polly pushed his hand away, 'I had no choice.'

Fable took Ishmael's knife from his cloak and held it towards Polly.

'I'm going to kill you now.'

'What? You're mad.'

'Indeed,' said Fable. Taking the blade, he cut a swathe of hair from her shoulders, then pressed the tip of the knife into her tummy button. 'Like you say, you have no choice.'

'Wait, stop.'

Fable hesitated; Polly took off her apron and unclipped her bra.

'Good, O yes, very good,' said Fable. He cupped a breast in one hand and held the knife at her throat. Pulling back his cloak, he pulled down Polly's knickers.

'No, not - please don't,' said Polly, the blade glinting in her eyes. Fable said nothing, entered her and forced her against the sink.

'Rejection,' said Fable as he increased his speed, 'makes me mad, Polly, you understand that don't you.'

Polly started to scream. Fable placed a hand over her mouth, thrust a final time and withdrew.

Polly stared at him, tears in her eyes, 'You bastard.'

Fable smiled, brought the knife down and sliced off the tip of her breast. Polly screamed and looked down at the raw grain exposed underneath. Fable swished the blade again, the tip of her other breast dropped and span like a top on the floor. Polly slumped to the floor; bubbles flowed from her mouth as she tried to speak.

'Enough, I'm bored,' said Fable and plunged the knife deep into her chest.

Fable looked at her as life drained from her body, then pulling his cloak back around him he strode out of the tent. The rest of the Punch and Judy gang were running up the beach. Fable glanced back at the tent. The two speakers bobbed in the air spitting and hissing at him.

'Game over, Lucifer Sam!'

Fable stuck his finger in his mouth. He blew hard, inflated his cheeks and lifted into the air. The speakers complained and thrashed as he reached out and unclipped them from their moorings. With their umbilical cords severed they fell silent. Fable blew the air from his mouth and descended. The speakers thumped lifeless into the sand beside him. He smiled a greeting as the gang drew near.

Static … crackle … pop.

Ishmael pushed the button again.

Static … crackle … pop went the speakers.

'Stupid car radio.'

Static … crackle … pop … the sound of opera flowed up the interior of the windscreen.

Static … crackle … pop … '-five miles of tailbacks to the drive through at Junction ten.'

Static … crackle … pop … '-We shall fight in the hills, we shall fight on the beaches.'

Isaac groaned at the noise. Above him the lamps along the central reservation stuttering into the distance lighting an ethereal runway for wayward souls as daylight faded. Isaac rubbed his eyes and looked at their yellow light folding across the crash barriers onto the motorway. He glanced up and saw an image of a man with his arms outstretched on either side of the light's crosspiece. Blue eyes looked down on the stream of traffic flowing by. Isaac shook his head and the image receded into the ocean of his mind.

Donaldson swam around the large cross beam of a lamp descending into the water. It sparked and sent shafts of light into the depths below him. He trod water for a moment and watched entranced as a thorn of crowns floated away over the surface, then kicked towards shore. Before him the cliffs divided the sum of the sky and sand, giving an infinite solution to Isaac's question repressed within Donaldson's mind. Donaldson reached the shore and stood up, the water of Isaac's sub consciousness trickled down through his black assault suit which absorbed the pain of Isaac's past into Donaldson.

Walking out through the waves, Donaldson looked at the pile of sentries lying before him; they stood contorted in their death throws into statues standing against the rise of the sea. Donaldson lifted one of the muskets and peered along the barrel. Framed in the sights he could see the man in the tatty red and black cloak who had spoken to him at the gravestones sitting in front of the Punch and Judy tent.

Donaldson removed the safety catch on his pistol and walked up the beach. Fable remained sitting in the sand staring at the tent. Donaldson dropped the musket, crept up and pushed the nozzle of his gun into the back of Fable's head.

'You tricked me,' said Donaldson, 'I should never have attempted to go to Gyrus.'

'O Hi, Donaldson,' said Fable, 'you're just in time, the show is about to start.'

'What?'

'The show, Donaldson, it's all about the show, sit down with me.'

'Where are the Punch and Judy gang, are they dead?'

'Lucifer Sam! Dead! No, well only a bit part player, the rest are on in one minutes time.'

'I have orders to kill them,' said Donaldson.

'Have you now?' said Fable, 'I think I can help you with that.'

'Like you helped me believe I should go to Gyrus to redeem Isaac?'

'Isaac, what is he? Sit.'

Donaldson lowered his gun.

'Hmm.'

Fable smiled. Donaldson sat beside him and pushed his gun into the side of Fable's stomach.

'How can you help me?' said Donaldson.

'I have-,' Fable paused and passed a plate of gingerbread men to Donaldson, 'Here try a saucerful of secrets.' Donaldson held his hand up in refusal. 'Suit yourself, I have put the gang in a trance to entertain me. I think you will quite enjoy it as they kill each other for us.'

Donaldson glanced up as a blast from a trumpet announced the start of the play; the flaps pulled away and Mr Punch appeared on the stage. Fable clapped his hands, 'O goody, it's started.'

Donaldson shifted in the sand, uncertain at a rerun of Isaac's childhood memory.

'Don't worry,' said Fable. 'I've altered the script somewhat.'

Inside the Ferrari, Isaac placed his hand on Ishmael's arm.

'Can we pull over?'

'What? No.'

'I think I'm going to be sick, Ishmael, please stop.'

Ishmael sighed, checked his mirror, indicated and pulled over to the hard shoulder.

Isaac got out. Before him loomed blocks of stone pierced by metal spikes that held back the earth from the channel cut through it.

'Hurry up,' shouted Ishmael over the noise of the traffic.

Isaac wretched.

He wiped his mouth on the back of his sleeve. Around him the sound of tyres spinning in lanes, wind and engines filled his head. He raised his chin and stared into the approaching headlights, a rabbit frozen by the spectre of death.

The lights flared up in his mind, the motorway cleared of traffic; the cat's-eyes running down the hard shoulder became flags fluttering in the breeze, the road a stage.

A cardboard cut out of Isaac's Porsche 911 appeared before Isaac. Mr Punch had his head in the open bonnet. He looked up past Isaac and said, 'Come on you old hag.'

'Be there in a minute,' came the high pitched voice of Judy behind Isaac.

Mr Punch looked straight at Isaac, winked, then ripped out the wires from the car's interior. He threw them towards him. Isaac stooped down and picked them up.

'That's the way to do it! That's the way to do it!' shouted Mr Punch as he closed the bonnet.

Judy pushed past Isaac with the baby in her arms and got into the car. Punch shut the door for her, walked around to the driver's side, got in and took the wheel.

'Off for a nice day at the seaside,' said Punch waving goodbye to Isaac.

The car pulled off, the baby bouncing on Mrs Punch's lap.

'Did you fix the brakes?' said Mrs Punch.

'O yes, dear,' said Mr Punch.

Isaac turned the wires in his fingers, 'The accident, I was responsible, it was my fault.'

'Isaac,' said Ishmael. 'Isaac, get back into the car.'

Isaac watched Punch and Judy disappear.

'Get back in the bloody car, Isaac.'

Isaac shook his head, sat back in the passenger seat and closed the door.

'What were you doing?' said Ishmael.

Isaac stared straight ahead along the hard shoulder.

'I didn't fix the brakes properly.'

'What?' said Ishmael.

'The crash,' said Isaac, 'It was my fault.'

'What do you mean?'

'I fitted the brake discs myself, saved myself a fortune.' Isaac sighed, 'Saved myself a fortune and lost my family. What a fucking mess up.'

'Isaac,' said Ishmael, 'you can't blame yourself. From what dad told me, it was the other cars fault.'

'He spoke to you about me?'

'Of course, he was always defending you against my hatred.'

Isaac fell silent.

Ishmael indicated and pulled back out into the stream of traffic.

On the beach, Donaldson watched as another car appeared on the other side of the stage. The blind man sat behind it.

'This seems familiar,' said Donaldson to Fable.

'Shh,' said Fable, 'You'll spoil the show.'

'O dear,' said Mr Punch. 'The brakes have failed and we are hurtling towards a car coming towards us.'

Mrs Punch turned and blew a kiss to Mr Punch, 'Don't forget me when we're all dead, dear.'

The two cardboard cars approached, the baby cried, 'Daddy, Daddy.' His head jerked forward at the impact, Mrs Punch shuddered and fell back limp. Mr Punch rubbed his head, looked at the blood on his hands, then looked across at his family.

'They're dead,' he shouted.

Fable burst out laughing.

'Are they really dead?' said Donaldson.

'O yes,' said Fable. 'Fantastic isn't it!'

The policeman entered from the right wing. He examined the blind man who sat in a pool of blood in his car, then at Punch holding his dead baby.

'What's going on here then?'

'I've killed my baby,' cried Mr Punch, 'It's my fault, I should have fixed the brakes.'

'Right,' said the policeman flipping open his little black book. He flicked past the sketches of Pretty Polly and found a space under a drawing of her lying dead on the floor, a blade through her heart. The image brought no feeling under the blanket of Fable's trance. 'You must come down the station with me. You've killed your wife and child.'

'No!' shouted Mr Punch, 'I'm going to take you down to hell.'

Mr Punch whacked the policeman on top of his head with his slapstick. The policeman collapsed, his skull fractured, blood spilled onto the stage. Fable laughed.

'That's the way to do it! That's the way to do it!' Punch sang out in his high pitched guttural voice and kicked Toby who was sniffing around the cars. Toby fell from the stage and landed in the sand in front of Donaldson.

Donaldson watched Toby manage to raise a paw, then turning his gun, shot him in the head.

'Good,' said Fable. 'You're entering into the spirit of it, splendid.'

Donaldson looked back at the stage, Mr Punch was beating the doctor over the head as he tried to attend to the fallen gang.

'That's the way to do it. That's the way to do it!'

'Damn,' said the doctor as he fell dying.

'You'll hang for that,' said Jack Ketch appearing with a noose. He slipped it over Mr Punch's head and started to lift Punch from his feet.

'You do understand,' said Fable as Punch squirmed free and pulled the noose tight around Jack's throat, 'with the gang dead you will be free of Isaac forever, Tom, you will forever be Donaldson.'

Donaldson nodded as the Devil ascended from a trap door in the stage floor.

'Death, death, the sentence is death,' said Fable.

'You've killed everyone, Mr Punch,' said the Devil. 'I have come for you.'

Donaldson flinched at the certainty of death conveyed in the Devil's words as they echoed around the beach. Mr Punch stuffed his fingers into his ears and launched himself at the Devil shouting, 'No, I have come for you.' Donaldson watched as they scrambled together over the stage and rolled off the edge.

Clouds of sand billowed up around Mr Punch and the Devil as they fought. Punch's slapstick rose into the air leaving in its wake clear sky in the swirl of yellow. The Devil arched backwards, his wooden form starting to split under the strain. Splinters appeared around his waist that stuck out through his shirt. The Devil flipped back up and drove forwards. A memory of his movements held in the flying sand behind him leaving a trail of sand devils. A cloud of rage tore through Isaac's mind. As it did, the swirling sand turned orange, then red. The force of blows increased until Punch flew backwards. He landed with a loud thud next to Fable.

'Get up,' said Fable. 'Finish it.'

Mr Punch turned to Fable.

'Finish it,' repeated Fable.

Mr Punch nodded, got up and picked up the musket lying in the sand. Turning, he raised the weapon and aimed it at the Devil's head.

BLAM.

The lead ball lodged in the Devil's temple; he fell dead. Mr Punch shouted with glee and jumped back onto the stage to take a bow.

'O bravo!' said Fable, getting to his feet to give Punch a standing ovation. 'Shoot him, Tom,' he whispered, 'here lies the only flaw in my plan.'

Mr Punch danced around covered in blood. Donaldson aimed as Punch bowed again. Punch raised his head and smiled a last time as his wooden head splintered from the bullet into the scenery behind him.

Inside Ishmael's car, Isaac let out a howling shriek as the last of the gang died. He fell forward onto the dashboard with a thump. Ishmael reached over and shook him.

'Isaac ... Isaac!'

Furrowed fields blurred past. Ishmael watched the flow of brown lines sweeping across the landscape. They looked like musical staves awaiting a tune from the earth.

On the beach, Donaldson looked at Fable dancing on the sand.

'What was in that for you?'

'Hmm...' said Fable. 'Let me think ... what is it that I want? Arh, yes, you see this...'

Fable twirled around on the spot and extended the flat of his hand. It connected with Donaldson's pistol and sent it flying. Fable caught it and laughed as his cloak billowed out around him in a blur of red and black.

'You see this zoo, Tom. I hate it,' said Fable spitting the word zoo out. 'I want to-'

Fable paused. He coughed and held his stomach as the words buried there surfaced. His cheeks puffed up as he tried to prevent their sounds from forming on his lips. With a gasp he spoke again, 'Apples and Oranges. O ... right then ... really? ... well apparently Isaac created me to personify the wonderful stories his dad told him as a boy, only now he has forgotten me. I'm to return to him and resurrect his childlike joy-'

Fable clenched his teeth shut. Tiny bubbles started fizzing out through his white barricade. Donaldson watched as the bubbles grew larger until one pushed up from the back of Fable's throat and forced his teeth apart.

'Effervescing Elephant.'

Fable spoke the words as the bubbles burst around his face. He wiped his mouth with the back of his sleeve and said: 'Hmm internal conflict. Sorry Donaldson, wanted to say ... he has forgotten me, so I shall take my revenge and pull Isaac into Hell where he will never be reunited with Rebekah.'

'And that leaves me free?' said Donaldson.

'Um, arh … no,' said Fable, 'naturally you are too strong a persona for Isaac to have available to him, you will have to die.'

'What?'

Fable stepped forward and placed a ring on Donaldson's finger.

'What the hell is that?' said Donaldson.

'O that,' said Fable, 'is Isaac's wedding ring, it will return you to your SAS friends at the airport.'

Fable swished his cloak around him. Tom saw inside as it billowed out. It was dark and filled with tiny lights. The medal holding it together glowed.

'Now is the time,' said Fable, 'now is the time you learn not to meddle.'

Fable ripped off Donaldson's mask, replaced it with a balaclava and said, 'With this ring I wish thee dead.'

Fable smashed the butt of the pistol onto Tom's head.

Darkness.

Fable stooped down, opened Donaldson's hand, placed his pistol in his palm and closed Tom's fingers around it.

Light.

Tom opened his eyes. He could hear Fable's voice ringing around his head …

-I'm coming for you, Isaac.-

Tom looked around. He was in a room, a metal bin on the wall, two people sitting in a corner. Outside he could hear feet pounding. The cocking of a pistol hammer.

BLAM. The door shook. CRASH. It flew open. CLINK. CLINK. A flash bang stun grenade scampered along the floor. BANG. The noise billowed out into the room. FLASH. A magnesium flame flared.

'Go.'

Tom watched himself enter through the smoke. Donaldson raised his weapon up and pointed at Tom's chest cavity.

BLAM.

181

BLAM.

Donaldson raised the pistol higher.

BLAM. The pistol kicked up.

The spent bullet shell span up out of the gun to join the two shells hanging in the air. The bullet clipped the edge of Tom's balaclava. The three shells fell to the ground and clinked against its hard surface; a soft thud filled the room as Tom fell clutching his stomach.

Donaldson walked over, kicked himself, and looked at the two civilians who had soiled themselves in the corner. He kicked Tom again.

Again, again …

Death fell around Tom and seeped in through the entry wound. His body pumped the coldness of it around his body and away from the torn edges of skin.

'I'm in the,' he said through blood lined lips, 'I'm in the past-' he looked down at the ring on his finger, then up at himself glaring at what it meant. The blade came, Tom screamed as he cut off his own finger.

'No.'

Shock waves.

'No.'

Pain crept into every part of Tom's body.

'Hold on, hold on.'

Pain ate at Tom's brains. It bit down around his heart.

Then it stopped.

Tom's mind left the confines of his body. He watched detached as dark blood pooled around the stub where his finger had been.

'Hurry you haven't much time,' said a voice.

Tom looked up and saw Bethuel, Rebekah's dead father, above him.

'What?'

'My daughter,' said Bethuel, '…do you love her Donaldson?'

'Yes,' said Tom.

'Then go to her, Tom,' said Bethuel. 'You know where she is.'

Tom looked at his dying body, then appeared inside the plane on the tarmac outside. The memory of Rebekah pregnant with the twins, sat looking out of the window, searching. She turned to Tom.

'Hello, Rebekah.'

'Hello, Tom.'

'I…' said Tom, 'This is all my creation.'

'Yes,' said Rebekah. 'It's very you.'

'Take this,' said Tom giving her his pistol. 'Use it to undo what I have done.'

Rebekah faded, the voices around Tom's fallen body played out the lines given to them…

'What the hell are you doing?' said one of the civilians.

'Shut the fuck up,' said one of Donaldson's team at the door.

Donaldson aimed his pistol at his future head and squeezed.

BLAM.

Donaldson's mobile started ringing again. He pulled it out; the screen was still dark. He placed it to his ear.

'Donaldson?'

'I'm coming for you, Isaac.'

'What the? Who are you?'

'Ha ha ha …'

CLICK.

On the beach, Fable walked over to Donaldson's dead body. He looked at the severed finger, then kicked him into the sea with the tip of his shiny black boot.

Tom Donaldson's body floated on the smooth surface of the water. Isaac's mind started to erase him. The water flowed over his face as he sank. The blue around him remained smooth. There was no disturbance on the water at his passing, only a silent shroud of death hovering, waiting.

Turning, Fable walked back towards the tent and disappeared inside.

In the centre of Mamre Wood the ground started to bulge as the water from the storm the night before bubbled up from the soil. The drops lifted from the ground and floated up into the air. They hung there forming a blue veil of water which shimmered in the light. A foot like that of a bear pushed through the suspended waterfall. A head followed. Then another and another until with a roar a creature stepped through. Its leopard like body was covered in black and white patches and its mouths were like that of lions. It searched around the wood with its seven heads and smiled.

The sound of distant singing rose up around the beast. It snaked one of its heads back through the water. The singing grew louder as if coming from someone running towards the spot from a great distance. The beast opened its arms and embraced the music as it swirled out from the veil and span up around its horns. The water droplets bowed outwards as if billowing in the wind. The veil broke and pierced the strange beast in a sheen of watery darts. For a moment it was lost from sight under the shafts of blue. And then it was done.

In its place stood Fable. He spat out the surplus water and stood blinking in the light. He removed his tattered cloak and threw the medal holding it to the floor. The medal lay there for a moment, then drained away into the ground. He glared up at the Dandelion Tree. Under the shadows of its branches the starlight within his eyes glowed; a part of his identity buried below his frosty expression; the eyes of Abe, Isaac's father.

Fable tipped his head back. A chilling laugh flowed out from him. It covered the wood in darkness.

Chapter 20
News From a Distant Land

Rebekah looked out of a portal in the upper levels of Temporal Gyrus, her thoughts a tourniquet to her blood, a strip of tape on her back giving answer. Below the memory of the shopkeeper from the hospital had set up store in front of the queue of memories. High above the Relic Monger screeched and swooped.

Behind her two sentries stood at attention either side of a circular steel door with a rusty locking wheel. Each had a musket against their shoulder. Rebekah pulled her blanket over her pregnant body and thought about her conversation with Deborah outside the gates of Temporal Gyrus:

'How many months?' Deborah had asked looking at Rebekah's pregnant stomach.

'Five,' said Rebekah.

'Are you Rebekah?'

'Yes, sorry who are you?'

'Deborah, your son Jacob is in the hospital I work at.'

'Excuse me?'

'Sorry, didn't you know?'

'What happens to him?'

'I, look sorry I shouldn't be talking to you.'

'What happens to my children?'

Rebekah rubbed her stomach as she felt the twins fighting in her womb and turned to the sentries.

'Can I have a glass of water?'

The sentries looked at her and sniggered.

'Does she know yet?'

'No, I don't think so.'

'What's so funny?' said Rebekah.

'You'll see miss, you'll see.'

Rebekah sighed. One of the sentries played with a pencil between his fingers, 'Would you like a clue?'

The other sentry laughed, 'Good one.'

A glow bled from around the door and played across the bottom of the room. Rebekah lifted a foot as her toes turned red in the light.

'He is here,' said one of the sentries. He turned the wheel; the noise of bolts radially retracting flowed out around them. The other sentry swam over to Rebekah and jostled her with his musket towards the door. It swung open releasing a stream of bubbles to the ceiling.

'There is no need,' said Rebekah, 'I'm not afraid.'

'You should be miss, you should be.'

Rebekah swam through into the inner chamber. Abimelech was before her, filling the room with writhing tentacles. One snaked out and curled around a basket of eggs in the corner. Abimelech selected one and brought it to his mouth. There was a cracking sound and a chirp as he swallowed. Feathers floated out around Abimelech's orbs that circled in a halo above his head.

'Hello, Rebekah, would you like a seagull egg? The chicks are at that tender age.'

Rebekah folded her arms over her bump, 'No thank you, Abimelech.'

'Hmm, well to business,' said Abimelech. 'You may be wondering why you're not incarcerated back within our high security ward after your romp with Isaac.'

'Because you show compassion to pregnant mothers?'

'Because, Isaac has been tempted and has succumbed to Fable's manipulative ways.'

'What has he done?'

'I'm afraid he has turned you over for a life of prostitution, Rebekah.'

'No, he would never betray me like that.'

'O, but he has, Rebekah. He has the two ingredients that are required. Fable provided him with the opportunity and he took them freely.'

'What?'

'He accepted you as a Playboy centrefold; that together with the newspaper he took completes the criteria for the transfiguration in Isaac's mind.'

'Shit.' Rebekah backed away. 'You can't. Send me back to my old cell.'

'Don't make a scene, Rebekah, it's actually a good idea. It is too upsetting for Isaac to keep remembering you; he will never look for you amongst the Temporal prostitutes.'

'No, let me go to him.'

'No – he's already killed himself because of you; I can't allow any more damage.'

Abimelech grabbed Rebekah around her ankle with a tentacle and pulled her into the air. Her blanket floated towards the floor revealing the smiley face on her naked body.

'That will have to go,' said Abimelech. 'Can't allow that in here, Rebekah, you know the rules.'

Rebekah struggled free and dropped to the floor.

'No you will not touch it,' she said and reaching behind her back she pulled Donaldson's pistol from the strip of tape. Grasping it with both hands, she pointed it at Abimelech. A dark shadow covered her body save a line of red from Abimelech. It traced up her right thigh lighting her crescent tattoo on her hip, swept around the outside curve of her right breast revealing a guardian star, and ran along her outstretched arm to end at the gun framed by her gold bracelets.

'Tom's gun,' said Abimelech. 'Now this is getting very interesting.'

Rebekah set her toes forward and locked her ankles to take the kick.

'I will escape,' said Rebekah. 'You can't hold me forever.'

BLAM!

A bullet streamed through the fluid, the pistol kicked and Rebekah stepped back into the shadows to steady herself.

'Stop,' said Abimelech.

The bullet glinted in his red light as it continued.

'Stop.'

Rebekah closed her eyes and willed the bullet forward.

A dull thud sounded as the bullet embedded itself in Abimelech's soft flesh. The two sentries swam in. Abimelech thrashed then fell silent as blood from the hole floated around him. His orbs fell onto the floor and grew dim.

'What the?' said one of the sentries.

Phicol and Ahuzzath, the other two custodians, appeared. The sentries raised their muskets and pointed them at Rebekah's head.

Rebekah emptied the gun's magazine into them.

The sentries' muskets floated to the ceiling.

Two sets of tentacles wrapped around Rebekah's arms; a green and blue glow painted stripes down her sides. Phicol and Ahuzzath looked at the body of Abimelech, then pulled Rebekah out of the room as a school of Neon Tetra fish swarmed around Abimelech nibbling the dead flesh.

The two custodians exchanged glances as the locks rammed home in the door sealing the death chamber. Behind them a battalion of sentries stood talking. Phicol turned and stared at them.

Rebekah found a footing in the darkness of her thoughts and visualised the custodians dissolving into the fluid around her.

Phicol looked as one of his tentacles fragmented into a thousand components.

'Take her,' said Ahuzzath as he and Phicol escaped in a flash of light.

Rebekah spat bubbles into the fluid around her and glared at the sentries.

They shrank back.

Rebekah stepped forward then fell as the butt of a musket rammed into the back of her head. The sentries shuffled up and rolled her over. She was unconscious. They got to work: one scrubbed the happy face from her stomach, others wrapped newspaper around her body. One tapped his pencil against his head and looked at the newspaper print.

'Hmm, where's the crossword?'

Another read the headlines, 'Woman killed by supermarket sociopath.'

The sentries sat down in a circle around her and started to read as the Neon Tetra behind the door wormed through to Abimelech's skeleton.

Rebekah fought through a fog of concussion and opened her eyes again. Looking around she screamed then willed the sentries to die. The sentries smiled toothless grins at her, 'Too late miss, the transfiguration is complete.'

Rebekah screamed again. A sentry reached around her, pulled the tape from her back and stuck it over her mouth, 'Shh love, we're trying to read.' Rebekah looked at him, her pupils dilated, breast milk smeared the print around her nipples, her unborn children fought within her.

Chapter 21
I Will Bring You Back to this Land

'No,' he thought. 'I will drown.'
'Open your mouth,' repeated the voice.
'No.'

...

...

Blurred images streamed past. They slowed to form a picture of a street. A flash appeared, sending up a spark. It twinkled as if the beating of tiny wings, then descended on an easterly wind onto a bank note lying forgotten in the gutter. A curl formed at its corner, with a flash, it flared up in a blue flame. The wind blew more notes from other streets towards the fire. The flame embraced them and danced finding a weakness in which to take foot.

The image streaked upwards.

...

...

'Open your mouth,' said the voice.
'I thirst,' he thought ignoring the strange voice in his head.
'Open your mouth,' repeated the voice.
'No.'

...

...

Again the pictures flowed as if a real of film speeding through a projector. A jolt, definition again showing a fire raging through the streets of London. The wind grew fierce and pushed walls of flames westward into the heart of the city. A voice from the roaring fire sounded out a death rattle. Clouds of bright yellow rose up like smoke from a furnace into the steel grey sky and billowed westward over the landscape. The river of flames below streamed after it, driven on by the howling wind. Lightning appeared and flashed down around the buildings. Loud peals of thunder sounded high above. Showers of fire drops rained down and helped the spread of the great fire. Piccadilly fell to its wrath,

Regent Street. Trafalgar Square stood against the advance until it too succumbed to the mounting flames and it seemed the city was without hope.

The image streaked upwards.

...

...

'You have a fever,' said the voice.

'I thirst,' he said.

'The fire will pass from you,' said the voice.

...

...

Cigarette smoke weaved around the ascending images, it lingered as the picture projected again into his mind. A dog resting on Whitechapel Road disappeared in a ball of flames. A car parked outside Bow Street vaporised in the intense heat. In an alleyway in Liverpool Station, an old discarded boot melted and oozed over the street. A top hat left jauntily at the edge of Park Lane, lifted up on the crest of a wave of fire; it span around as it spiralled upwards and disappeared. An old iron, thrown onto the street in Pall Mall, steamed and fell through the road as the surface around it melted.

The image streaked upwards.

...

...

'Do not fear,' said the voice.

'I am scared,' he said, 'my daddy has left me.'

'Do not fear,' said the voice.

...

...

The images gained definition again, bringing sight, smell, noise. The stench from the houses wafted up over the devastation. Their melted green forms oozed around the streets. Red gloop from the burnt hotels flowed into them until they swelled to form large rivers of hot plastic. The rivers flowed towards the heart of the city. There they came together and formed a lake of fire. The heat increased and yellow flames started to dance over its surface.

A metal ship slipped forward from Old Kent Road into the depression and sailed across the lake. Its strong bow cut through the red sea. The dancing of the flames quickened and tongues of fire flickered up over her deck. She sank nose first and disappeared.

The image streaked upwards.

. . .

. . .

'It has passed,' said the voice.

'It is dark,' he said.

'Light comes,' said the voice. 'Open your mouth.'

'No.'

. . .

. . .

An image of a large tree descended and stopped. A long ladder dropped down.

'Climb,' said the voice from out of the darkness.

'Why?'

'I want you to see me,' said the voice.

The climb was long. Crocodiles grinned as the figure ascended. His lungs were empty. He had little time. It had seemed that way forever. He rested, yet resisted the urge to open his mouth. He had been drowning for too long to give up now. He wasn't about to flood his lungs. He wasn't ready to leave. Not yet.

'Climb,' said the voice.

Small fingers grasped the last rung. A hand reached down and pulled him up. The face of the boy stared up into the face of a man which shone with the brilliance of the sun.

'You can hear my thoughts can't you?'

'Yes. What is your name?'

'Jacob.'

'Your name shall no longer be Jacob, it will be London.'

'I saw London burn.'

'Now open your mouth,' said the man.

'No. What is your name?'

'Why do you ask my name?'

'Am I dead?'

'Yes, you died a few moments ago. Now obey and open your mouth, London.'

Jacob started to cry.

'I don't want to die, I have held on for so long. I want to go home. Please can I go home?'

'London, do you believe in me?'

'Yes.'

'Then open your eyes,' said the man.

. . .

. . .

Inside the hospital room, Jacob opened his eyes. He watched as a shimmering outline of the man hovered outside the fractured glass of the window. Translucent wings beat up and down on the man's back; singing followed their rhythm and drifted through the hole in the glass. The image fluttered in the air, as if paper blown on the breeze. With a snap it stopped and formed what looked like the chalked outline of a dead body in a crime scene. The sound of singing grew louder, air became flesh, silence to breath.

Smiling, Gabriel stepped through the window. Ripples of atmospheric music followed him from the glass as it vibrated in harmony from his passing.

'Hello, London.'

'Hello,' said Jacob his mouth and eyes wide at what he had witnessed.

'Your mouth is open,' said Gabriel.

Jacob placed his hand over his mouth. Gabriel reached down, peeled back the hand and touched Jacob's mouth. Dry lips started to open. Water poured inside; Jacob gagged. Gabriel placed the glass back on the bedside table, then placed both his hands either side of Jacob's shoulders. He looked into Jacob's dull eyes; a glint started to rise, the glint became a sparkle.

'I'm thirsty, can I have another drink please?'

'Now get up, London,' said Gabriel.

Jacob floated up from the bed, leaving his dead body behind.

'Are you God?'

'To answer that will take too long, London. Come.'

'What happened to me? Why am I here? Where are my parents?'

'There are many questions and I will answer all that I can as we travel, but now we must go.'

Gabriel scooped Jacob up in his arms and smiled at him.

'I will explain some of what you must know on route.'

'Where are we going?'

'We have a train to catch,' said Gabriel, pushing the window frame up.

The sound of music filled the room. Gabriel held Jacob close. They stepped out of the window and lifted up into the sky.

Back in the room, the picture of the Playmate stuck to the wall fell away. It fluttered to the floor, a leaf shed to mark the end of a season.

Chapter 22
The Days to Come

The sun was low. Its rays broke against the old trees along the road and flowed up their wrinkled skins. Ishmael looked at the soft yellow glow of the trunks and glanced up at the blue fingers of their cold branches forming a canopy over him. As he drove towards Mamre House, the light flickered on and off through the gaps in the trees. Ishmael's world went into strobe. Some things along the road became clearer, others disappeared in darkness.

Ishmael drove past Mamre House and pulled right, onto the path next to Stubble Face Field. His Ferrari struggled on the track, yet it accepted the rough treatment. The sound of a didgeridoo floated up from his stereo as the car entered the wood. The tyres crushed a path through the sea of bluebells nestling up against the narrow path; branches scratched into the shiny surface of his car.

Ishmael turned his head to Isaac; he was still unconscious.

'Come on, Isaac.'

Isaac eyes fluttered. He groaned and sat back up.

'Hold on,' said Ishmael. He placed his hand on Isaac's shoulder, 'Everything is going to be okay. You're going to make it.'

'I just want to fall into bed,' said Isaac.

Laban crashed through a bed of leaves in a large clearing in Bethuel's Leap and walked up to a black statue of a headless horse.

'Is this it?'

'No,' said Jidlaph, 'but we are close.'

Laban looked at the horse; it stood on its hind legs with its front hooves raised into the air. On its flank was a small black and yellow Ferrari badge. A black rider sat on the horse's back, a long bow in his free hand, a crown on his head. Clipped red grass broke the fall of the shadow from the statue. Decking encircled the lush grass in a circular ring of blue; an arc of myrtle trees provided the backdrop.

'Wow,' said Laban. 'Who'd have taken you as a landscape gardener?'

'Laban that is The Statue of Conquest, not a garden ornament.'

Laban looked at the horse again.

'But it is black. Doesn't a black horse symbolise famine?'

'That is the time we live in, Laban.'

'What do we do when we find this hidden memory, Uncle?'

'I have to download it into Isaac's mind as the last of the sun's rays fall on Mamre Wood.'

'Why?'

'I don't know.'

'What is the memory?' said Laban.

Jidlaph started to answer then stopped as he felt the cold touch of snow on his nose. He glanced up. The sky was white.

'What's happening?' said Laban.

'Strange,' said Jidlaph, 'We're back in a spring section, not winter. It shouldn't be snowing.'

Laban turned his head upwards; the snow fell in thick flakes covering the lane in a blanket of white. He felt the cold dash of winter on his cheeks; warm air from the nostrils of the horse rose as it turned from black to white; the colour of conquest.

'I think,' said Laban staring at the horse, 'that the season is about to change.'

Jidlaph turned to the white rider.

'Is it much farther to this memory?' said Laban.

'No,' said Jidlaph, 'It's just a short way down the lane from here.'

'I'm cold,' said Isaac rubbing his hands together in Ishmael's car.

Ishmael looked at him. Isaac had turned a pale blue. The white of his eyes seemed flat and pale.

Ishmael drove past one of the great sycamore trees forming a circle around the clearing in the centre of the wood.

He looked up at the Dandelion Tree. It rose strong and tall into the reddening sky. The wood took on a magenta hue under the fading canopy. The red light flickered over the blades of grass so they appeared to be flames swaying back and forth in a gentle breeze. The fire parted before the Ferrari as it approached.

Ishmael stopped the car and got out. The long shadow of the Dandelion Tree stretched over him. Ishmael walked around to the passenger side of the car and helped Isaac out. Isaac leant on Ishmael's shoulder to support himself and peered up at the tree from his past. He felt light-headed, as if his cares were floating off his shoulders into the branches above.

The two brothers walked towards the Dandelion Tree. Ishmael's arm around Isaac, their footsteps heavy on the ground.

They stopped at the sound of twigs snapping. Fable stepped out from behind the Dandelion Tree and stood before them.

'Hello, Isaac.'

'Who are you?' said Ishmael.

'Lucifer Sam, Isaac! You've aged badly.'

Isaac looked at Fable, 'Do I know you?'

'You used to,' said Fable. 'A long time ago.'

'You look familiar,' said Isaac. 'Are you here to help me? Did Gabriel send you?'

'Yes, right,' said Fable. 'Here to help you take control.'

'What?'

'Where is Rebekah?' said Ishmael.

'I have her,' said Fable.

'What?'

'Take me to her,' said Isaac.

'Gabriel said nothing about you,' said Ishmael, 'what have you done with her?'

'You long for her don't you, Isaac?' said Fable.

Isaac nodded.

'You have a deep sadness,' said Fable, 'To be with her again, well then the Champagne will flow over your loins, cookies will drip from your kisses, daisies will sing as you make love.'

Ishmael stepped forward and placed himself between Fable and Isaac.

'Isaac, this isn't right. Something is wrong.'

'Desist, Outcast! Be quiet and silent. Are you hungry, Isaac?'

Fable reached into his pocket and took out a bright red apple.

'This is a fruit from the Dandelion Tree. Eat it and you will walk with Rebekah again.'

Isaac examined the apple.

'Hurry Isaac or I will offer it to Ishmael. He has desires.'

Fable flicked his gaze and met Ishmael's eyes.

Ishmael started to open his mouth to protest.

'Would you deny yourself your inner desires, Outcast?' said Fable.

The light dimmed further and struggled to find its way into the clearing. Isaac looked at the ring of fallen daffodils, then stepped forward with legs of stone and reached out his hand. Fable smiled as Isaac took the red apple.

'I don't want to feel this pain anymore,' said Isaac turning to look at Ishmael. He bit into the apple.

'No,' shouted Ishmael. 'No!'

Fable laughed. The leaves from the Dandelion Tree started falling from the branches high above. They floated down around Isaac and settled at his feet. Fable stepped back. One of his black boots crushed the head of a daffodil lying in rest on the cold ground. His other boot started to smoulder as the red grass lapped over it.

'What,' said Ishmael grabbing Fable around the neck. 'What have you done?'

Fable reached into his pocket and took out a crumpled piece of paper.

'According to the instructions the next choice falls to you.'

'Shut up. What have you done to Isaac?'

'He has chosen a path back to the past that will lead him into a despair so great that he will be lost forever.'

'What the hell are you talking about? Where's Rebekah?'

'I can't tell you yet, the rules don't allow for such a cast of the dice. Now, Outcast, your turn to place a footnote in Isaac's history. Kill your brother now whilst you have the chance.'

Ishmael narrowed his eyes and tightened his grip around Fable's throat.

Unseen around them two armies of fiery horse drawn chariots stood together in a circle. Ishmael's army drew back black arrows on their long bows. Isaac's drew their blue swords. Ishmael felt for Isaac's knife in his pocket, then released it again.

'I have forgiven him. I will not strike my brother.'

'Arnold Layne! What a shame, you don't want to play.'

'You see this all as a game?'

'Pow R. Toc H,' said Fable and with a flourish of his arms he pulled the water from the ground beneath him into the air. Fat globules of water swirled in front of him. They bumped into each other and came together to form a thick spherical wall of water wrapping around Fable. Ishmael looked at the distorted image of Fable through the watery veil. Rebekah appeared inside the bubble beside Fable. Fable pulled her towards him, kissed her.

'Leave me alone,' said Rebekah.

Fable moved a hand behind her head, played with her hair, then taking the blade he slowly drew it down under her eye drawing a trickle of blood.

Rebekah screamed. Ishmael stepped forward, 'No.'

Fable smiled and pushed the knife against her throat.

'Stay back,' said Fable. 'I need to send her to Hell at the appointed time.'

Ishmael slammed his hand against the blue wall.

'No.'

Isaac looked up as emerald leaves fell around his head. They felt soft and warm and he welcomed their touch. He stared up into the tree as the leaves fell around him like rain and breathed in their sweet scent. The leaves became smaller and transparent. Isaac watched as colours seeped away. He saw his reflection in them as they started to curl in on themselves to form clear spheres. It was a reflection that washed away many years from his face; it was smoother, his hair thicker.

Isaac felt the cold touch of water swirling around his toes. He heard the sound of a choir singing far away in the distance. A violin played over the angelic voices. The singing grew louder and became the sound of falling water. Isaac looked up again and saw the leaves had become dewdrops pouring down over him. Above the evening dusk had changed to a pale blue hue. Isaac listened to the drumming of the water and looked ahead.

In front of his face was a plastic screen, misted over. Isaac glanced down at himself; he was naked, his stomach tighter. He raised his hand and opened his fingers out against the screen. Sweeping it around in an arc, he rubbed away the condensation leaving a clear impression of a moon in the mist.

Behind it was the face of his wife. Isaac gasped. The mist cleared; Rebekah stood with a pale blue light illuminating her naked form. On her stomach was the happy face. Under her eye was a small scar.

His heart pounded out her name within him Rebekah-Rebekah-Rebekah-.

The dewdrops became the patter of hot water from a showerhead above. The drops thudded down over his skin and trickled down his legs.

'Come on, Isaac,' said Rebekah, 'what are you doing in there?'

'I-'

'And what is this?'

Rebekah pointed to the happy face on her tummy.

'That? I, O God, Rebekah, I love you.'

'Then you can help wash it off cheeky.'

Rebekah opened the shower door and stepped in. Isaac looked at her. She wrapped her arms around his neck and kissed him. Stepping back under the water, she passed him the sponge, 'Come on then.'

Isaac smiled and scrubbed her pregnant stomach. Black and yellow paint streamed down her legs. He lifted the sponge and sent bubbles streaming down over her. Rebekah's nipples hardened; drops of water splashed down from their tips, as if springing from two diving boards.

'This can't be real,' thought Isaac as Rebekah turned before him. He washed her back and then reaching around her, cupped her breasts; they felt solid, their mass entwined with gravity to form weight in his palms.

'Not dreaming then,' thought Isaac.

'You been daydreaming again?' said Rebekah.

'Hmm?'

'You live with your head in the clouds,' said Rebekah spinning to face him. She pulled up close.

Isaac could feel her bump against his stomach. He tried to blurt out again his love for her; she silenced him with another kiss. Reaching down she wrapped her fingers around him and guided him in through the spinning soapsuds.

Rebekah and Isaac shifted against each other, two pieces of driftwood bumping together on the incoming tide, trying to find a rhythm in the confines of the cubicle; Rebekah's bottom pressed against the plastic, her bump protesting.

In Mamre Wood Rebekah squirmed under Fable's grip as he pushed her hard up against the Dandelion Tree. Isaac stood in a trance lost in the past. Ishmael was shouting.

Golden leaves started floating down with the water in the shower. The pitter patter of the water in the cubicle changed into the voice of the choir again. Isaac heard the words to a song flitter through his mind ...

Under the Dandelion Tree the two lovers met,
Wonders explained, their paths are set.
They run naked before parting in sorrow,
With despair in his heart he returns from tomorrow.
Among the trees of the garden they once ran free,

Now they separate again,
Under the Dandelion Tree.

'Please don't,' said Rebekah as the tip of the knife pierced her skin.

Ishmael gritted his teeth and pushed his hand against the water. It gave way and he started to break through.

An image of a bear appeared next to Fable as the tips of Ishmael's fingers reached towards him. Ishmael continued to push. The blue of the water seeped away from the edges of the hole, leaving a clear concentric ring of fluid around Ishmael's arm.

Fable watched as a drop of Rebekah's blood ran down the blade. Bubbles appeared around the inner curve of the wall where Ishmael's fingers protruded. Ishmael felt the warmth flow out from them. He held firm, muttered a prayer and continued to push. Seven heads wrapped around Fable and glared at Ishmael. There was a sudden jerk, a rush of bubbles, a loud swoosh. The wall exploded into tiny droplets; the beast disappeared.

Knife entered flesh, Rebekah grasped and fell.

In Isaac's trance, Rebekah fell limp in his embrace. The water turned red.

'Rebekah!' screamed Isaac. He turned her and looked at the cut at her throat.

Rebekah went into soft focus. Music from a violin flowed over the hum of the shower pump. The water drops became colder. They turned green and unfolded into soft leaves.

The fading light from the evening brushed down over the face of Rebekah. Fable turned to face Ishmael. Rebekah's body lay slumped to the ground. Drops fell over Fable's shoulders and seeped into his body; he started to grow taller as his form took on the extra water. Laughing, he lifted his hand against Ishmael.

Ishmael's hand shot out and held back the blow. Fable struggled to free his arm.

Ishmael looked at Rebekah then, with a cry he slammed Fable against the Dandelion Tree. A loud CRACK echoed around the clearing. Water started dribbling out of Fable's mouth as he slipped down the corseted trunk. Bubbles span around his lips. The stars in his eyes rose to the surface and started to flicker. Ishmael looked at them and for a moment he thought he saw his father. Fable fell forward with a soft thud onto the red grass. His body started to steam where the blades touched him.

'Ahh,' cried Fable. He struggled back to his feet. 'Lucifer Sam! All I ever wanted was to be loved. All I wanted was to be able to play with Isaac.'

Fable paused and peered into Ishmael's eyes.

'You used to play with him didn't you?'

'Kind of,' said Ishmael.

'Do you miss-'

Fable coughed and spat some water from his mouth.

'Do you miss those childhood days?'

'I regret how I spent them,' said Ishmael.

'Yes, yes,' said Fable. 'Regret.'

Fable glanced at Isaac who stood blinking under the falling leaves.

'I am mad you know,' he said. 'Been that way for years.' He started to weep. His bright colours drained towards his toes.'

Fable stopped as the dark unseen fingers of the beast reached into him. He shook his head and smiled, 'I win the game, Outcast.'

Ishmael drew his father's blade from his pocket.

Fable started to snarl. The army of archers behind Ishmael pointed their arrows towards the Dandelion Tree.

'Forgive me,' said Ishmael.

'Put away your toy knife you bastard child,' said a distant voice from Fable's lips.

Ishmael drove the blade into Fable's chest. Fable looked down as the knife entered him, images of Polly in his mind. The noise of a thousand blue arrows filled the air as Ishmael's archers unleashed their weapons, as they had done before against his brother. Fable fell back as the arrows thudded into him. Sap dripped from the tree where they struck around him.

Fable struggled to hold his form as the light in his eyes grew dim. With a sigh the bubbles lost their cohesion and Fable slipped from the bed of arrows. He fell in a shower of water droplets. The drops sat on the red sea of grass for a moment then, one by one they seeped down around the Dandelion Tree. The sound of a saxophone lifted up from where Fable had stood. It played a slow lament as it floated up into the sky. Turning the two armies rode off into the wood.

Ishmael studied the patch of ground where Fable had fallen. Turning, he grabbed Isaac and started to shake him.

'Isaac, snap out of it. Isaac!'

Ishmael's hands started to flow through Isaac as Isaac's body started to fade.

Ishmael stared up the crocodile ladder, 'Get down here and get your hands dirty.'

Isaac shuddered and then looked down at himself. He was clothed in the green hospital gown again. It was wet. The thin material failed to absorb the chill of the evening air around him. Goosebumps pushed up against the itchy cotton. Isaac leant over and wretched.

Before him, Ishmael sat cradling Rebekah in his arms.

Isaac stood back up and wiped his mouth.

'Rebekah!'

Ishmael looked up at his brother.

'She's gone, Isaac.'

Isaac walked to her and stroked the side of her cheek.

'Rebekah.'

Tears fell.

Isaac started to fall.

Ishmael put his hand out to steady him, Isaac's feet buckled.

'Isaac,' cried Ishmael.

Isaac tried to answer; the pain from his chest constricting his words. He looked up into the face of Ishmael; above them the sky burned red.

Isaac fell onto the grass and lay staring at the trunk of the Dandelion Tree rising up before him.

Laban looked around as the late hour stole away the daylight from the white world around him.

'We're here,' said Jidlaph.

Jidlaph stooped down and picked up a rounded pebble from the river. He looked at the glistening stone, then put it in his slingshot. Pulling back his sling, he took aim. Laban peered down onto the path waiting to see what memory carried such importance.

A bubbling noise brought his gaze back towards the trees. The beech tree before him swelled up, as if being pumped full of water. Laban's world slowed …

Branches twitch and writhe…wooden fingers crack and release their grip.

Beech bark ruptures…shafts of wooden skin shoot outwards, danger within.

A loud rumble…snowflakes skim across the path on the wave of sound and dive into the river.

A cry…the hard noise of the pebble falling onto the lane reaches upwards in vain at the ascending balloon.

Isaac's voice…

Awake from slumber Old Man Willow,
Castellan of yore, open up your path of darkness.
Take me into the comfort of my night,
Lead me into the madness of folly, broken delights.

Laban tried to clear his mind from the screaming within. Beside him Jidlaph clutched at a branch piercing his body; a trickle of crimson blood flowed from the edge of his mouth. The branch twitched and lifted Jidlaph off his feet. Laban watched as Old Man Willow swung Jidlaph up into the air. Drips of blood fell and splashed into the snow. Jidlaph writhed for a moment, then with a sigh fell still.

Old Man Willow shook him and retracted its arthritic fingers with a snapping sound. Jidlaph's dead body fell into the river. Laban looked at the disturbance over the surface of the water. Old Man Willow stepped forward towards him. Bark cracked and sparked at the unnatural movement.

'You killed him,' said Laban. He collapsed onto the lane, 'I'm never going to see him or Rebekah again.'

'I am here,' said Old Man Willow, 'because of you, Laban.'

Laban turned, 'What?'

'Because of you, Rebekah is lost.'

'You're lying.'

'Isaac placed me here after your wagging tongue alerted the custodians. It is here that your father died, and it is here that you will now join him.'

'No,' said Laban.

He stood up and faced Old Man Willow.

'I am a bounty hunter,' he said. 'I wonder what price for you?'

Laban held his lighter up before him and blew on the flame; it flared up into the sky. Old Man Willow shrank back. Laban picked up a pebble from the path with his free hand.

'This is for Jidlaph.'

Laban let the pebble fly. It drove up through the falling snow and pierced the membrane of the ascending balloon.

The balloon burst with a POP! Old Man Willow shrieked.

The image floated to the front of Isaac's mind ...

Fade In.
Scene 7: Ext. Mamre Wood, Year: 1968 – Day 7

ISAAC *is a boy. He sits under the Dandelion Tree. He is starting to search for a meaning to everything. He recalls the laughter on the beach when he was five, yet is confused as to why he can no longer sense that lightness again. He has many questions. Is* GOD *there? Does he love me? If* ISHMAEL *can be sent away, could the same happen to me?*

ISAAC   God. If you're really there. If you really love me. Then move the tree to show me.

ISAAC *looks up and stares at the tree willing it to move. It remains still. He gets up and tries to shake it with his hands.*

ISAAC   Move!

ISAAC *climbs up the crocodile ladder. He looks up. There is nothing there.*

Fade out …

Isaac looked at the Dandelion Tree as the memory faded. He had checked it again each morning for a week afterwards. Nothing had happened. He had started to doubt. Doubt had grown to frustration. Frustration had sown seeds of disbelief.

As Isaac turned towards the patch of ground where the tree had once stood, the pain in his chest subsided. Getting up, he hobbled over to the fallen daffodils. He reached down and touched one. As he did, the last ray of light faded and the colour drained away from the grass under his feet. Isaac lifted his gaze and noticed the new position of the tree, to the right of the ring where it had once stood. Isaac stepped towards it. He reached out and touched the smooth warm bark.

'This is ridiculous,' he said.

He peered up through the branches. With their fingers blackened in the twilight, they arched up in sharp contrast against the pale sky. Points of light started appearing within their embrace as the stars started to shine.

'I'd given up believing it. It's taken him over thirty years to answer the foolishness of a boy. Thirty years!'

'Take Rebekah to the top of the tree,' said Ishmael.

'What?'

'Take her, Isaac,' said Ishmael, 'It is your only hope.'

Isaac looked at the tree again, then at Rebekah. Reaching down he picked up her limp body and placed her over his shoulder.

'Climb,' he said to himself and placed his foot at the bottom of the crocodile ladder.

Chapter 23
The Great Fire

The statue of the Temporal prostitute gleamed in the courtyard. Golden sheets of newspaper detached themselves and floated away leaving her untarnished by the history of yesterday's deeds.

Far above her, the two remaining custodians looked up as fear plunged uninvited into their eyes. The stream before them played images of the coming end.

'Old Man Willow has failed us, we have been out manoeuvred.'

'We will stand against the onslaught,' said Phicol.

'It would be futile,' said Ahuzzath. 'We should pray to the golden statue.'

'No,' said Phicol, 'Raise the drawbridge to the portcullis.'

The two custodians turned, and headed down to the parking lot.

Above Temporal Gyrus, a fire flowed down through the blackness of space. Plunging through the pale blue upper atmosphere of Isaac's consciousness, it poured over the neuron skyways weaving around the sky prison, and gathered around the dark halo of the parking lot. The custodians floated at the barrier, a pile of sandbags under the wooden arm of the entrance and watched the wall of flames approach their world.

The fury stormed the entrance. Thousands of splinters streamed outwards as the barrier shattered. The sandbags flew in all directions. The flames hit the custodians with such force they span up as if origami creations blown on a wind. They writhed and fell burning in agony to the ground. The fire stripped their flesh and ate into their bones then leaving them, rose up over the neon HM TEMPORAL GYRUS sign over the portcullis. The letters glowed, sparks flew, words melted. The flames rose up farther and poured through the portals peppering the outside of the prison.

The hundred blue doors in the courtyard burst into flame as the fire swirled around the stone pillars and licked around the feet of the golden statue. As it rose up pink arms formed at her shattered shoulders. She spluttered, coughed, then fell. Rebekah pushed her way through her burning door and looked around at the other prostitutes running through the flames. Spotting the fallen girl at the centre of the courtyard, she ran across; the print of *Woman Killed by Supermarket Sociopath* burning.

'Come, Mahalath,' said Rebekah and helping her up to her feet led her through the open portcullis.

Once she was sure that Mahalath was safe, Rebekah ran back and stopped before the hole in the middle of the courtyard. White flames shot up through the opening and rose into the air making a roaring sound. Rebekah pushed her fingers into the fire and watched the flames flicker around her fingers, then stepping off the edge, she dropped down into the fury.

Below memories flew around in panic, noise and the smell of burning meat assaulted Rebekah's senses until she had to drop to the floor to continue. She coughed, peered through the smoke and saw him. Esau sat with his bowl of lentil soup on his lap, his eyes wide open in fear. Shouting, Rebekah got to her feet and pushing through the madness scooped him up in her arms. Holding him tight she let herself be caught up with Isaac's fleeing past until she once again passed through the portcullis. She held Esau close to her skin to protect him from the heat and from being swept from her. When finally she reached the edge of the parking lot, she paused and looked back. Behind her HM Temporal Gyrus burned, black soot spiralled upwards. Turning, Rebekah placed her hand over Esau's eyes, pushed through the outer membrane and leapt from the edge into the waters below.

At the end of Bethuel's Leap the dead body of Jidlaph brushed up against the roots of the Dandelion Tree pushing into the river from the bank. For a moment he lay there entwined with only the noise of the water breaking the silence. Then a slow ballad sounded; Jidlaph's body lifted from the water and rose in the music towards the arc of the tree's branches.

Rebekah splashed down into Isaac's consciousness; her newspaper floated across the water and the smiley face reappeared on her stomach. A white light glowed around her. She rose again, younger and clothed in a pure white wedding dress, blue confetti floating down, church bells ringing in her ears.

As Isaac climbed the Dandelion Tree, he looked at the wood below them; it was lit by the bright full moon. The light streamed down through the branches and bathed the long grass in a pale white light. The light grew brighter in Isaac's eyes, his eyelids started to flutter and in his mind's eye he watched his memories of Rebekah play before him. The images coloured in blues and greens, flickered like pictures from an old film reel. The flow of her past grew faster, then stopped. Church bells started to ring. Rebekah appeared clothed in a pure white dress. In Isaac's mind a flash of white blazed as he broke through to taste, smell and cherish her; blue confetti floated down over their laughing faces.

Isaac looked up at the white stars thrown across the open sky and continued to climb.

Chapter 24
Isaac and Rebekah

The glow of the terminal bled into the sky to light the wings of passing people. Snow fell and dusted the train as it left the protection of arced plastic like a pig leaving its sty to forage for truffles. Isaac looked out of the window as the station pulled back, then glanced at his Rolex. Around him, people sat with paper drawbridges waiting for the track to lead them to supper, children, wives, mistresses. The train picked up speed and with a sigh the driver picked up his paper. Behind him the length of the day brought fatigue across evening faces.

Beside Isaac, an old man's head bobbed with the rhythm of the train; his newspaper coming close to his eyes then receding again with each nod.

The train slowed and stopped at a station. Isaac put his book down and took a bite out of his chocolate.

The carriage spat out a few morsels, then ate whole those waiting to board. Doors shut behind them like the toothless gums of an old woman. The train pulled away from its concrete harbour leaving rows of marked graves.

Isaac checked his watch again then opened his book. Splinters of glass tumbled over the black type. The stale smell of sweat pushed out of the seats impregnated by the overfed buttocks of businessmen and seeped around the carriage. Above their heads the electric arms of the train rose to connect with the overhead cables. The train danced along the track following the line.

Inside his head, Isaac could hear singing. The voices sang of wheat, clear skies, north winds. Isaac could feel his chest rise and break as the tracks fell before the wheels of the train. His pulse increased and he felt a sensation of falling, laughing.

Isaac glanced at the woman and child sat opposite.

The woman lowered her book and for a brief moment their eyes met. Isaac looked away, then up again. As he looked at her he felt a burning desire, a joy connected. He remembered tears searing the storm, the heat of the sun, a kiss of consummation.

'Tickets please.'

Isaac put his hand inside his jacket pocket and produced his pass. The conductor clipped it and handed it back. Isaac watched the woman pull her tickets from her book. He glanced at her left finger. A ring.

'Thank you,' said the conductor handing back the bookmarks.

Isaac looked around; papers became barbed wire, suitcases rabid dogs, overcoats: vultures flapping in the overhead storage rack. Isaac sucked in his imagination, inhaling it as if nicotine to his soul. He breathed out. Heads nodded, vultures snapped, dogs barked.

The woman opposite smiled at him and ruffled the hair of the boy beside her who sat eating a pop noodle. The dying light streamed through the window to play over her hair and caress her face. As Isaac looked at her he could hear the ticking of his body clock and he shifted in his seat to try and still his mind against the aftershock of battle.

The woman turned a page, then coughed.

A ruffle of paper distracted Isaac from his thoughts. A man next to the woman had dropped his paper and fallen asleep with his head pressed against her chest. Isaac looked at the saliva flowing from the man's open mouth. The woman pushed him upright. He flopped back.

'Let me help,' said Isaac.

The woman nodded and smiled. Isaac leant over and tipped the man towards the cold comfort of the window. The sleeper grunted and sucked up his dribble like a man slurping froth from a beer.

'Thanks,' said the woman.

'No problem,' said Isaac. The woman continued to smile at him. Isaac felt the tip of her foot brush up against his inner thigh. The evening disappeared as the train went through a tunnel. Isaac became aware of the throb of wheels over tracks underneath.

'Have you forgotten again, Isaac?' said the woman.

Isaac looked at her.

'Sorry?'

'It's me,' said the woman, 'and your son, Esau.'

Isaac looked at the woman. As he did her light registered in his mind.

'Rebekah? Esau?'

'You have to concentrate,' said Rebekah. 'Your mind is still fragile.'

Isaac got to his feet.

'We made it to the top of the tree?'

'Yes and we danced together in the great hall, remember now? You span me around to the music.'

'And the food,' said Isaac, 'the banquet – Esau, you drank all the soup!'

Esau put his hands around his father and hugged him.

'How can you still be hungry?' said Isaac looking at the pop noodle.

Rebekah smiled.

Isaac stepped across to her and touched her fingers. Rebekah's eyes shimmered and she laughed. Isaac took her up in his arms as he felt the connection drawing them into the sky.

'We're on our way?'

'Yes.'

'Truly?'

'Yes, Isaac, you, me and the kids, a new life.'

Isaac laughed then picking Rebekah up he kissed her. A man on the other side of the train straightened his paper and tutted.

'I waited for you,' said Rebekah. Isaac kissed her again, smiled and continued in his laughter.

'Where's Jacob?' Isaac asked as he slumped back into his chair, 'I don't remember Jacob at the party.'

Rebekah raised her finger to his lips, 'Shh it's okay here comes London.'

Other Titles From Cauliay Publishing

Kilts, Confetti & Conspiracy *By* Bill Shackleton
Child Of The Storm *By* Douglas Davidson
Buildings In A House Of Fire *By* Graham Tiler
Tatterdemalion *By* Ray Succre
From The Holocaust To the Highlands *By* Walter Kress
To Save My father's Soul *By* Michael William Molden
Love, Cry and Wonder Why *By* Bernard Briggs
A Seal Snorts Out The Moon *By* Colin Stewart Jones
The Haunted North *By* Graeme Milne
Revolutionaries *By* Jack Blade
Michael *By* Sandra Rowell
Poets Centre Stage (*Vol One*) *By* Various poets
The Fire House *By* Michael William Molden
The Upside Down Social World *By* Jennifer Morrison
The Strawberry Garden *By* Michael William Molden
Poets Centre Stage (*Vol Two*) *By* Various Poets
Havers & Blethers *By* The Red Book Writers
Amphisbaena *By* Ray Succre
The Ark *By* Andrew Powell
The trouble With Pheep Ahrrf *By* Coffeestayne
The Diaries of Belfour, Ellah, Rainals Co *By* Gerald Davison
Underway, Looking Aft *By* Amy Shouse
Silence Of The Night *By* Sandra Rowell
The Bubble *By* Andrew Powell
Minor Variations and Change *By* Graham Tiler
The Darkness of Dreams *By* Pamela Gaull
Spoils of the Eagle *By* Alan James Barker
When I followed The Elephant *By* Tony R. Rodriguez
Calvi Sinners *By* Roberta Vassallo

Titles Coming Soon

Grassmarket Blood *By* Bronwen Winter Phoenix
The Psychic Biker Meets The Ghost Hunter *By*
Paul Green and Stephen Lambert
The Crownless King *By* Phil Williams

Lightning Source UK Ltd.
Milton Keynes UK

178659UK00005B/1/P